Don't Let Him Go

by

Kay Harris

I Want Morrison, Book One

Don't Let Him Go

Cover Art by *Kristian Norris*

The Wild Rose Press, Inc.
PO Box 708
Adams Basin, NY 14410-0708
Visit us at www.thewildrosepress.com

Publishing History
First Champagne Rose Edition, 2018
Print ISBN 978-1-5092-1950-6
Digital ISBN 978-1-5092-1951-3

I Want Morrison, Book One
Published in the United States of America

I folded my arms across my chest

and glared at Jack as he moseyed into the room. "You ambushed me."

Jack came to a stop a few feet away and nodded. "I did."

"That's it?" I spread my arms out and leaned forward. My voice rose despite my effort to control it. "That's all you have to say?"

"What do you want me to say? You're smart. You can see what I did back there. I used you for my own gain."

"You're a prick!"

"I'm not surprised you feel that way. But I *am* sorry you had to get caught in the crossfire." He moved to the couch and took a seat in the middle of it, purposefully giving me the high ground.

He slung his arms over the back of the couch casually, making him look like an arrogant ass. And that is exactly what I thought of him at that moment. So I called him on his supposed apology. "Are you?"

"Yes, I am. But you're not innocent, Candie. You put yourself in this position by going to work for Morrison."

"It's Candace!" I shouted, on the edge of insanity.

He didn't respond. He just looked at me with that infuriatingly handsome face and waited, an amused look dancing on his face.

Dedication

This book is dedicated to those who stand up for others.
You are the heroes that make our world a better place.

Chapter 1

Present day—Berkeley
Candace

"You're a mess," my best friend says to me.

Well, at least she's honest, and maybe a little kind. Way worse than a mess, I constitute a national disaster. My apartment falls in the same category. A week's worth of dishes fills the sink. Laundry lies about in bizarre places, including on top of the fish tank and in the bathtub. My coffee table strains under the weight of dirty cups, notepads, paper plates, and romance novels.

And me, I sprawl on the couch, covered in a blanket, wearing pajama pants and a T-shirt, practically unchanged since I came home six days ago to cry my eyes out and give up on life.

"You found me," I say. I sound unhappy about it. But I'm not.

Grace picks her way through the war zone and finds a chair to delicately perch on. "Seriously? What the hell is going on? I waited for you at the airport, but you never showed. You refused to answer the phone. Meg's out of town, in LA right now, doing a show. But when I got hold of her, she freaked. She said she hasn't heard from you in days. So, I came over here. And what do I find?" She throws her hand around the room, swiveling her head from side to side. "This is crazy,

Candace!" She frowns at me. "I'd hug you, but I have a feeling you smell."

"I'm glad you came. Really, I am," I say truthfully. "I…I need help."

"Clearly."

"How was the cruise?"

"Really? You wanna talk about the cruise?" She stares at me incredulously. "What the hell happened to you, Candace?"

"You were gone a long time," I tell her, shifting on the couch for the first time in hours. I wrench myself into a sitting position and look over at her. "You missed a lot."

Grace's husband, Eric, has a high-powered job with a high-powered company. She follows him to all these exotic places where he gets stationed on temporary assignments. Not only does the company pay for all their living expenses, he also makes a ton of money. Grace doesn't have to work at all, which leaves her free to jet set around, shop, and in general enjoy her life.

For the last six weeks, Grace has been on some exotic extended cruise trip by herself. She called it her "healthy marriage break." I was supposed to pick her up from the airport last night. She intends to stay at the condo she and Eric keep in the North Bay until he comes back from his current assignment overseas.

She invited me to join her on the cruise, but I turned her down because I'd just started an incredible new job that was supposed to provide me with a killer salary, amazing prospects, and all the happiness I could imagine. Now I sit here in front of her, just six weeks later, nearly broke, newly unemployed, and completely heartbroken.

"I'm sorry I stayed out of touch for so long," Grace says with genuine regret on her face. "When I got on that ship, everything seemed fine."

"I'm just glad you're here now." I sniff.

She makes her way over to the couch and leans down to hug me. When she stands up, she puts her hands on her hips. "Why don't we get you showered?"

As if I am an invalid, Grace gets me cleaned up, changed, and fed. We're just polishing off the grilled cheese sandwiches she made when she finally pushes me.

"You need to tell me what's going on. For starters, I'm guessing you haven't been to work." She looks around the apartment as if for emphasis.

I shake my head. "I quit," I say meekly.

"Because?" she prompts.

I let out a little sob and hang my head in my hands. "It's too pathetic. I can't say it out loud."

Grace scoots her chair around the table and puts an arm over my shoulder. "Sweetheart, you've got to tell me. What the hell happened?"

"A boy. I mean, a man. My life is in ruins over a man."

Grace stays silent for a long beat. So I look up at her. Her mouth is dropped open, and she's staring at me.

"What?"

"I just…I'm just…shocked," she admits. "I mean, Candace, *you*, completely wrecked over a guy. This is…unprecedented."

"I know," I say weakly.

"He must really be something," she breathes.

3

I rest my head on her shoulder. "He's...God, yes...he's really something."

"Well, where the hell is he?"

"Gone. He's gone." I wave my hand in the air. "Just like my job. Just like all the joy in my life."

"Okay, overdramatic," she says, lifting my head off her shoulder and forcing me to look her in the eyes. "Why don't you start at the beginning. How did you meet this guy? Who is he? And what the hell did he do to get you to crawl out of your little Candace cave and fall for him? And what on earth does all of this have to do with your job?"

I take a deep breath and tell her everything...

****

Five weeks ago—San Francisco

I stared up at Kent in utter disbelief. "You want *me* to represent John Morrison Jr.?"

"It's less of a 'representation' job and more of a 'babysitting' job," Kent said. He leaned toward me, amusement clear on his face. The jackass sat on the edge of my desk, one loafer swinging wildly. He was happy to be dumping this on me; it was written all over him.

"The son of John Morrison Sr., the freaking boss?"

Kent nodded again. "The very same asshole."

Dumbfounded, I twisted my hands together in my lap and considered that. I had only worked at the very successful real estate firm of Morrison and Sons for three weeks. They were giving the youngest and most inexperienced of our substantial legal staff an assignment involving the boss's son. It didn't make sense. So I had to ask, "Why me?"

Kent started to look uncomfortable. And I knew

something was up. I was a nobody, fresh out of my bar exam. Hell, the main reason I had this job was because they wanted someone young and inexperienced, which translates to inexpensive. My excellent references and grades, combined with the fact that my heritage helped to diversify the place a little, had all been considered major bonuses when they'd hired me. Still, I might be good, but I hadn't done anything yet to distinguish myself.

So, yeah, I was suspicious. There had to be something wrong with this assignment.

Kent shrugged. "This is part of paying your dues. The newbie always gets the shitty assignments." He looked down my blouse.

I leaned back to obstruct his view while chewing that over. If this was considered a bad assignment, I needed to know why. "And?" I prompted.

"I've had to deal with this asshole for two years," he said, a scowl on his face. "But I got rewarded for it," he said, almost as an afterthought to sweeten the pot.

It was true, though. Having worked for the company for just under three years, and showing no real promise as a good attorney, Kent had just been promoted and given a giant raise and a nicer office. He also got a new secretary. I got his old office, his old salary, and his old secretary. Apparently, I was also getting his old assignment.

I decided to drop the skepticism and approach this project with enthusiasm. After all, I wanted to make a good impression here. Sure, Kent wasn't my boss, but he was senior to me, and he reported everything to my actual boss. I needed to put on my happy-to-do-whatever face. "So tell me about him. What's the scoop?" I asked, a lilt in my voice.

He dropped a thick file folder on my desk. It made a deep slapping sound. It was almost ominous. "It's a basic babysitting job. Everything you need to know is in here." And then, just like that, he stood and headed for the door.

"Wait, Kent, that's it?" I called.

He turned in the doorway and smirked at me. "Read the file. You can ask me questions. But don't expect me to spend a bunch of time helping you out. This is your burden now. I'm done with it."

Then, he walked out of my office.

****

Three hours, several stacks of paper, and a few phone calls later, I had figured out why no one wanted this assignment. John Morrison Jr., who went by Jack, had broken with his family, big time. The oldest child of John Sr. and Margaret Morrison had turned his back on the family business at the age of twenty.

At the time, he'd been attending Stanford, pursuing a degree in business. Everything indicated he would follow in his father's footsteps. But then Jack dropped out suddenly. He disappeared for a few years and resurfaced two years ago as the president and CEO of a nonprofit organization he started with his own trust-fund money.

Jack called his organization Homes Without Inc., as in without companies, aka incorporated entities. It was cleverly subversive, I supposed. An advocacy group for people living in poor neighborhoods that were being gentrified, the organization targeted development companies, like the one Jack's family owned, and protested against them.

"Candace, your mother is on line one." Janice's voice came through the speakerphone, crisp and clear.

I repressed my sigh and hit the button. "Hi, Mom."

"You're still coming to dinner, aren't you, sweetheart?"

I glanced at my watch. Damn, it was already six thirty.

"Yeah, Mom. I'm leaving the office now. I'll be there by seven."

"Good, and oh, honey, I don't know if I mentioned it, but I have a guest coming."

I let out my breath. Of course, she did. "Okay, Mom. I'll see you soon."

I reorganized the papers in front of me, placing Jack Morrison's arrest record on top. No stranger to the police, he had been arrested numerous times for protests, standing in the way of bulldozers, and lying down in the street to stop traffic. Each time, Kent had gotten him out of any real trouble. In addition to bailing the rebellious son out of jail, Kent had also tried to tamp down the publicity caused when Jack protested his own family's business transactions. And now this jerk was my responsibility.

Before leaving the office, I took one last look at my email. I had a new one from my boss, Tom Garrity.

Candace,

I hear Kent got you up to speed on Jack. I think you'll do great with the little ingrate. Remember your main job is to keep the brat out of jail. He's indicated lately he plans to target Grover and Co. The DA's cousin owns Grover, and the DA is out for Jack's blood. My advice: keep his focus on us and off Grover. Do whatever you have to. All other assignments are secondary to this one.

Good luck and feel free to pick my brain for ideas.

Tom

Insane! My job consisted of keeping this moron focused on trying to destroy *our* company and prevent him from hurting the competition. Meanwhile, I had to try to keep him out of the press and out of jail. Kent was right; this really was a babysitting job.

****

Half an hour later, I sat at my parents' dining room table, if you could call it that. It was a handmade rectangular wooden object on legs that my grandfather put together from a kit forty-five years ago. And dining room was probably too nice a word for the small space that sat between my parents' tiny, outdated kitchen and their cramped living room.

"You look really nice, Candie," my dad said as he scooped a pile of cooked carrots onto his plate.

To say I was overdressed would be a major understatement. My father, who'd toiled away for the last thirty-two years as a public defender, wore his work clothes as well. But unlike my designer suit, his was an ugly tan color, featured no tie or double-breast, and looked like it had been purchased at Target.

"Honey, you always dress so nicely," my mother said, trying desperately to keep the criticism out of her voice.

She wore a knee-length sundress with giant flowers printed all over it and a pair of Birkenstock sandals, hardly appropriate for a woman in her fifties.

But my "date" was in the worst shape of all. He was a couple years younger than my twenty-five and good-looking. But no amount of chiseled features and doleful brown eyes could help the scraggly hair, five o'clock shadow, and dirty jeans and T-shirt ensemble.

"Yeah, Candie, you look great," Toby said, his mouth full of half-mashed green beans. I shuddered.

I still held out hope that someday my parents would wake up and realize who I was. As their only child, I knew it was hard for them. My mother's three miscarriages after having me sealed my fate as the apple of their eye and the sole focus of all their child-rearing attention. But I might as well have been adopted for all I had in common with my parents.

My father, a white upper-middle-class kid from the Peninsula, had turned his back on the stability that would have come with joining his father's law firm. Instead, he'd gone to work in the San Francisco public defender's office, lived in a shabby apartment, and joined the good fight for human rights.

That's how he'd met my mom. Young, black, angry, and idealistic, she'd come to the Bay Area from Seattle, where she'd grown up one of five kids to an activist preacher and his fiery wife. They'd collided like asteroids and lit up the sky. And they still glowed, even now, all these years later.

I may have been the result of their passion and love, but I was nothing like them. Ever since I was a little girl, I wanted to trade in my parents' Castro-district brownstone for a North Bay mansion. I wanted to wear designer clothes, not resale-shop specials. And I didn't want to spend my weekends being paraded around at protest rallies and demonstrations with a miniature sign and a cute slogan-bearing T-shirt.

I tuned back to the conversation as Toby said to my mother, "I'm going to be right there with you, Lily. I can't wait to see the looks on the faces of those greedy bastards."

Whatever crazy new protest they were talking about, I'd been blocking it out completely. But now my father addressed me. "What do you think about the referendum against evictions, Candie?"

Crap. I did not want to talk about this. It was a trap. So I played dumb. "Um, well, eviction referendum?"

"Come on, Candie," my dad said. "You must have heard about it."

Of course, I knew about it. My job as a corporate lawyer for a real estate company meant me and my coworkers were knee-deep in the fight *against* the evictions referendum, which would change the rules about when new landlords could evict existing tenants. If it passed, my company would lose a lot of time and money. And, of course, my parents, being the activists they were, supported the referendum wholeheartedly because it would help keep poor people in premium housing units in the city. So, the last thing I wanted to do was discuss it with them.

"Robert, leave her alone," my mother said in a half whisper.

I sighed. "Dad, can we talk about your disappointment in me later?"

"Candie," my father said sternly, "I am *not* disappointed in you."

But I knew that wasn't true.

Toby was confused. "What am I missing?" he asked.

He annoyed me just to look at him, with his purposefully messy hair, his I-just-don't-care slouch, and get a freaking razor, for crying out loud.

"Candace just started working for Morrison and Sons," my mother said casually.

"Really, Candie?" Toby said, his tone dripping with disapproval.

Oh, sorry, dude. I don't work at Starbucks like *you*.

"My name is *Candace*," I said fiercely. "And actually, I just got a new assignment today. I'm going to be representing *Jack* Morrison."

"No kidding?" my dad asked, dropping his fork.

"Really?" my mother added, clearly pleased.

"Wow," Toby said. "That's cool."

"Um, well, that sounds interesting," my father said. "Why would someone from Morrison and Sons be representing Jack?"

"Well, 'representing' isn't exactly the right term," I said, hedging a little. "More like working with him to keep him out of trouble."

"You mean out of the way," Toby said.

Before my fantasy of smacking him in the jaw with the wooden spoon sticking out of the roasted squash had ended, both of my parents gave him dirty looks.

"No," I said casually. "Not really. My job is to keep him out of trouble. John Morrison Sr. is paying me to keep his son out of jail, out of the sights of other companies, that sort of thing."

"I bet Jack is thrilled about that," my mother said softly.

Despite my mom's reservations, my dad had a different take on it. "Well, if anyone can keep Jack Morrison on the streets fighting the good fight, it's you, honey," my father said, beaming with pride.

In that moment, I was glad I'd been given this assignment. For once, I would be doing something that connected me and my parents on a deeper level than our basic genetics.

However, I would come to regret it all when I met Jack Morrison two days later.

Chapter 2

Trying to set up an appointment with Jack Morrison by phone or email had gotten me nowhere. The emails went completely unanswered. And the secretary, who sounded about twelve and chewed gum in my ear over the phone, was absolutely no help. After two days of getting the runaround, I took matters into my own hands and went down to Jack's office.

Located in an old warehouse, the office had been converted into open-concept lofts to accommodate tech start-ups. It was very San Francisco-y, with a killer location in the SOMA district on the edge of the Tenderloin.

As soon as I got out of the cab, I stepped on a pair of soiled men's briefs. I managed not to throw up while scraping off my pricey heels on the edge of the sidewalk. The stupid building had no elevator, and as I climbed the thousand-year-old concrete steps, I wondered if it was quake ready. But then again, it had probably survived the great quake of 1906.

The offices of Homes Without Inc. sat on the top floor. I had to admit they enjoyed a great view. But the view wasn't of the Bay, Alcatraz, and the Wharf, like my office. It showed off the seething city, the high-rises, old tenement buildings, and in the distance, the iconic capitol dome.

The office had *hippie* written all over it. The

moment I stepped inside, the sickening sweet scent of incense assaulted me. It made me want to gag. I hoped to God I didn't have to spend the next two years working with a guy who reeked of weird spicy scents.

Framed posters hung all over the walls. Most of them were demonstration flyers, blown up and made artsy. Others displayed the faces and quotes of famous activists like Martin Luther King Jr., Rosa Parks, Norma Rae, and Cesar Chavez. My eyes paused on a poster featuring the women of the Supreme Court.

My parents had forced me to read about all the women who'd broken through barriers, crushed glass ceilings, and fought for all that was right and good in the world. Of all those amazing women, there was one I'd always looked up to the most. As the first woman to be appointed to the Supreme Court, securing unanimous confirmation by the Senate, no less, she'd broken the glass ceiling I personally identified with on the deepest level. So I took a moment for my gaze to pause on Sandra Day O'Connor. She had, in part, inspired me to study the law. And now here I was, confronting her on a mission I never thought my law degree would bring me on.

I turned away from Sandra and examined the office space itself. I stood in front of what I assumed served as a front desk, though it was unoccupied. Various workspaces scattered about ad hoc around me, none of them enclosed with walls or partitions. Some people used those crazy stand-up desks. Others sat in groups at long tables. Dotted between the rectangles lurked a few round tables that reminded me of kindergarten arts and crafts time.

About two dozen people worked there. The

diversity would have received far more praise from my parents than the corporate offices where I toiled. But, whether or not the gender and racial dynamics more closely matched my parents' friends and the environment I grew up in, I was far less comfortable with these idealistic activists than my suit-wearing compatriots over in the financial district.

All of the employees were engaged either with a computer or another person. But a young blonde woman finally took notice of me and came over to where I stood by the front desk. Instead of going around to the back of the desk and greeting me from there, like a normal professional would, she flip-flopped over to me, a ridiculous smile on her face.

"Hi, can I help you?" she chirped.

"I'm looking for Jack Morrison," I responded, all professional and distant.

She considered me for a moment, then frowned a little. "Jack, someone from 'the company' is here," she called over her shoulder.

With that declaration, every pair of eyes in the place turned to me. I realized I was obvious. I wore a pale peach suit with matching heels. My medium-length hair was tied up tightly in a bun. And I carried a leather briefcase. The people around me had all dressed for work in jeans and T-shirts, though the girl in front of me at least wore a sundress.

At work my clothing fit in; it was my color that usually stood out. Here, I matched about a third of the people in skin tone, but none of them in any other way. And they noticed.

After a few beats of uncomfortable silence, one of them moved. He had been leaning over behind someone else, looking at the computer screen over her shoulder. But he stood and moseyed toward me, like he had all the time in the world.

He looked like a combination of an old-school hippie, a disillusioned GQ model, and a Greek god. He wore a pale-blue cotton button-down dress shirt just wrinkled enough to show he might take the care to pull it out of the dryer right away, but not care enough to iron. The rolled-up sleeves exposed his arms below the elbows and the unbuttoned collar allowed a peek at a sculpted chest. His jeans, despite being worn and tight at least didn't possess any holes. To top it all off, a pair of sport sandals covered his feet.

His too-long hair hung around his ears and just above his brow in a messy tousle that made him look like he'd just rolled out of bed, where he'd left two beautiful women, run his hands through his hair, and posed for a poster. He had incredible bright blue eyes, high cheekbones, and a regal-looking chin covered in a dark, sexy five o'clock shadow. That, combined with his thin but muscular build and well over six-foot stature, made him drool-worthy.

Please don't let this be Jack. There were no pictures in the file, and I didn't watch the news. I didn't actually know what Jack Morrison looked like. Maybe this was his insanely hot assistant or something.

"Hi, I'm Jack," he said, holding out his hand when he reached me.

Shit.

I took his hand. "Nice to meet you, Jack." That's right, I went informal right away. It's the best way to handle hippies. And, hey, I know how to handle hippies. I've spent my whole life around them. "I'm

Candace Gleason."

Jack dropped my hand and gave me a crooked smile. "Really? Robert Gleason and Lily Kincaid's daughter?"

So he knew my parents, or at least he knew *of* them. This could bode well for me.

"Yes, that's right. I've been trying to set up a meeting with you. Do you have time right now?"

"How do your parents feel about you working for Morrison?"

I smiled at him. "I'd be happy to talk about my parents with you during our meeting. Is now a good time? Perhaps we can talk in your office."

He grinned at me. And that was when I realized I should have known he was a Morrison because he looked like his younger brother, Hayden. I'd met Hayden twice during my short time at Morrison and Sons. Fresh out of college, he worked as a vice president or some such thing he was totally unqualified for. He, too, was good-looking and had that playboy grin. But he didn't quite have it going on the way his big brother did.

"This *is* my office," Jack said, spreading his hand out.

I scanned the room and saw that every damned one of his employees watched us intently.

"Okay then, can we sit down?"

He paused for a minute, and I thought maybe he was about to say no and kick me out. But instead, he smiled and said, "Of course."

He turned and started walking deeper into the office. I followed him. We passed a couple of the stand-up desks, a long rectangular group desk, and finally came to a stop at a kindergarten table.

Jack took a seat and gestured for me to sit beside him. I placed my briefcase flat on the table and sat down gingerly. Somehow, this environment made me feel really out of place, especially in my suit.

"Would you like coffee or water?" Jack asked.

The room was still very quiet. Everyone could hear us. It was so open, so strange. I had to find a way to get him out of here so we could talk.

"Coffee sounds good. Perhaps we could go to a shop. I think I saw one across the street."

I hadn't actually been paying attention when I'd arrived. I'd been too busy dodging street people to notice. So I wasn't positive there was a coffee shop across the street, but, hey, we lived in San Francisco—it was pretty much a given.

"No need. We have great coffee," he said. Then he got up and walked away from me.

Alone at the table, I swiveled my head around to take in my surroundings. Most of his employees had turned back to their computer screens now. But conversation had not resumed. They definitely planned to eavesdrop.

Jack returned with two cups of coffee in ceramic mugs. He handed me one with the dates and image from Burning Man two years ago imprinted on the side. I suppressed an eye roll.

"Cream?" Jack asked.

I did like cream, but afraid he would take off again, I shook my head. "I don't know if you've had any contact with Kent Bookman recently," I began.

Jack sat back in his chair and laughed.

I pushed on. "But I've been assigned to take over

his duties as they relate to you."

I had practiced this language for two days. How did one say "I'm your new babysitter" to a grown man? I thought I'd done pretty well in the delivery.

Jack took a sip of coffee and studied me. "I tried to fire Kent for two years. I suppose if I try to fire you, it won't do me any good either?"

I stared at him, confused. "Fire him?"

"I even tried getting a restraining order against him. But I'm sure you can imagine how well that went."

"Why would you do that?"

Jack leaned forward. "You're new. Right, Candie?"

"Candace," I corrected. Maybe he did know my dad. Why else would he call me Candie? Why didn't my dad tell me they were friends? "And, yes, I am relatively new with the company," I admitted.

"So, let me fill you in on a few things. My grandfather was a nice man. I sat on his knee as a little boy, and he told me stories and made me smile. But he was a bastard as a businessman. He started a business whose sole purpose is to make money on other people's misery. My uncle's all right, and my dad is a nice man." He shrugs. "He loves his wife, he loves his kids. Blah, blah, blah. But my dad was complicit when he went to work for my grandfather, and now he's in charge of the bloodsucking company."

He leaned away from me, some of the intensity gone. He took another sip of his coffee. "So, I know exactly what's going on. And I know why you're here, Candie. The question is, do you?"

I was speechless. I had absolutely no idea how to respond. I took a sip of my coffee as well. It was high-end stuff but strong as hell. I tried not to make a face.

I took a deep breath. "Well, I guess we're on the same page then. I work hard, Mr. Morrison, and I'm sure, as you can imagine, I want to make a good impression with your father. So I will do what it takes to fulfill my mission. And no, firing me or calling the cops on me won't get rid of me."

There, I'd laid down the law. Now we could get down to business.

Jack gazed at me and he looked—oh no—he looked amused. "You never did answer my question. How do your parents feel about you working at Morrison?"

I wanted to ask him how he knew my parents. But I needed to keep the upper hand here. "I think we should go over your calendar," I told him, pulling out my iPad. "I'd like to meet with you prior to any major events, protests, press conferences, and the like."

Jack laughed aloud. He was definitely amused. "I tell you what, Candie, why don't you come by tomorrow around one?"

Jack stood up and pushed his chair in. I scrambled to shove my iPad back in my briefcase and stand, too. I didn't want the meeting to be over just yet, but I felt like I'd made progress since he'd agreed to meet with me the next day.

I followed Jack through the office and over to the stairwell, the only private spot in the whole place. For the first time since we'd met, we were alone. And we stood there, staring at each other in the dim light.

"Thank you for your time, Jack," I said, holding out my hand.

He didn't say anything but took my hand in his. He

gave it a firm squeeze and smiled at me.

"I look forward to seeing you tomorrow," I said.

Jack still had my hand, and he pulled it toward him and leaned in. And that's when I knew he did not smell bad, not at all.

"It's been my pleasure, Candie."

"Candace," I said weakly.

He grinned and released me. Then he turned and walked away.

Chapter 3

"Dad, I was wondering how well you know Jack Morrison," I asked.

I'd decided that before my meeting with Jack, I might as well get as much intel as I could. So I'd called my dad as soon as I got home that evening.

"Hmmm," my dad responded. "I can't say I know him well. I did meet him at a rally your mother was running a while back. Lily," he yelled away from the phone. "Wasn't Jack Morrison at the Civic Center station rally last June?"

I did the math; that was almost a year ago. It wasn't the kind of close friendship that would likely have led to my parents talking to Jack about me. But I had to be sure.

"Your mom is almost certain he was there," my dad told me.

"So…um…did you talk to him?"

"I probably did, honey. I don't remember."

"Did you talk about me?"

A long pause settled between us before he answered. "Honey, I love you, you are my princess, and I am so proud of you," my dad said. Just the words made me blush. "I don't want you to take this the wrong way, but I don't usually talk about you to strangers at a rally."

I felt like laughing. Of course not. Calling me

Candie was just something Jack did to throw me off. He didn't do it because he'd had some cozy relationship with my father. Feeling spiteful, I wondered what Jack would do if I started calling him John Jr.

"Oh, I just wondered," I told my dad. "I mean, he knew exactly who I was and who you guys were and everything."

"We're all part of the same community of activists, Candie."

"What do you know about him?" I probed.

"He's a pretty interesting fellow. From what I've heard, he grew up a true rich boy. Lived in a mansion, went to a fancy boarding school, jet-setted around Europe, the whole bit. And then suddenly, in college, he just disappeared. Five years later, he showed back up in San Francisco and started a nonprofit with his family's money. He's always saying he uses the blood money from Morrison and puts it to good use. Some people criticize him for using family money, but I think he has a point. If he just rejected that trust fund, refused to take it, it would go to his sister and brother who are both involved in the company."

"So, aside from that, is he well respected in the activist community?"

"Oh, definitely," my dad said. "He's fierce, determined, and not afraid of anything. Plus, a lot of people respect that his main target is his own family."

I didn't respect it. I didn't respect it at all. I had nothing in common with my parents, but I would never torpedo them. As far as I was concerned, it was wrong.

My dad interrupted my thoughts. "Your mom wants to talk to you."

Before I knew it, my mother was on the phone.

23

And I knew what she wanted to talk about even before she said it. "So, what did you think of Toby?"

"You know, Mom, for a feminist, you are awfully determined to make sure I'm tied to a man," I told her.

This wasn't the first time we'd had this conversation. But my mother had fallen madly in love with my father. Their love had nurtured her dreams. And she truly believed that, if I found my soul mate, he would only lift me up, not hold me back. What she didn't understand was my soul mate couldn't be found at one of her "free the people" meetings down by the docks.

"You didn't like him," she said, just barely suppressing a sigh.

"Mom, I don't have anything in common with him."

"Candace, having things in common is not necessarily the key. It's all about spark, sweetheart."

"Mom, I promise to do my best to keep my eyes open for that one special person in the world," I said to appease her. "In the meantime, I need to focus on my career."

She sighed. I knew it killed my parents that I'd taken this job at Morrison and Sons. But they were the ones who'd spent my entire childhood telling me to follow my dreams. And having a high-powered position as a corporate attorney at a prestigious firm like Morrison and Sons *was* my dream.

"I gotta go, Mom. Tell Dad goodbye for me."

"Okay, sweetheart. Love you. Talk to you soon."

I hung up feeling no closer to a revelation about my new project than I did when I left Jack's office that morning. I decided to make myself something to eat, feed my fish, and go to bed early. I wanted to call Grace, but she'd gone off the grid, on a freaking boat ride somewhere. I knew from a text I'd received earlier in the day that Meg was out on a date. I was alone.

After dinner, instead of going straight to bed, I ended up Googling Jack Morrison. I got a ton of news articles about his protests and his arrests. Jesus, this man was constantly being hauled out of places in handcuffs. There were also editorials he wrote lambasting his own father's company.

I switched over to Google Images and found about a million pictures. The ones from the last two years all focused on Jack at protests or press conferences. But there were also images that went back farther, all the way back to Jack's childhood.

There were a few family portraits mixed in there. These featured John and Margaret with their three children, professionally done, well groomed, and perfectly posed. My favorite was taken when Jack was about twelve. He stood next to his father. John Sr.'s hand perched on his shoulder. His mother sat just in front of him, Chelsea, at about five or six, on her lap, and Hayden, who would have been around nine or ten, to her side. Jack looked adorable, innocent, but with the clear markings of a boy who was on his way to being a handsome man. He smiled a very genuine smile.

Pictures of him in his teenage years showed a developing playboy. He started to get a sneer on his upper lip. His light brown hair sported a surfer-boy streak of blond. He wore a cloth bracelet on his wrist.

There were also a handful of pictures from his two years at Stanford. One showed Jack at eighteen, looking for all the world like a kid with no cares. The sneer on his upper lip was even more pronounced. His bright blue eyes shone with the confidence of a young man who had everything and could get whatever he wanted.

But another picture, taken just before Jack disappeared, was very different. Gone were the blond highlights and the sneer. Instead he looked sullen, defeated. The striking blue eyes were still beautiful, but sad.

Then, there were the five missing years. No pictures existed from that time. And the online articles I could find about it were all speculation. Some claimed he'd gone on an extended trip to Europe, others said he'd hid out in the Amazon rainforest, and one report claimed he'd gone walkabout in the Australian Outback.

One thing was certain: when Jack Morrison returned from wherever he'd been, he had changed drastically. Lean, muscled, and tan, there was a hardness about him. Gone was the softness of wealth, a feature that could still be seen in Hayden.

I could not deny I found Jack Morrison attractive. In fact, he was the first man in a long time I'd paid any attention to. Law school and the part-time job I'd worked all through it had taken all my energy over the past three years. When I'd graduated, I'd focused on passing the bar and finding a "real" job, a feat I had just achieved three weeks ago. So, now I was settling down. And in settling down, I noticed men again. That was all there was to this. It had nothing to do with Jack Morrison specifically. Right?

****

The stupid man had appeared in my dreams, which made me already cranky with him. And then he'd left me standing there, in front of his vacant front desk, waiting.

I'd arrived at Homes Without Inc. a good twenty minutes early for our one o'clock meeting. But rather than pay any attention to me, Jack huddled up with his staff in the far corner of the office. He'd waved at me briefly after I'd been there for about ten minutes, but that was it. Irritation rose up my spine.

Actually, I'd been annoyed since the moment I'd opened my eyes that morning. Too much Internet gawking was surely to blame for the dream I'd had last night. In it, Jack leaned over me, shirtless, caressing my face. That was it, just a half-naked Jack caressing my cheek, his face leaned in close to mine. It was bad, sure, but not so terrible really. Except that in the stupid dream, we were lying in bed.

I'd tried to get rid of the image, I really had. I'd listened to music while I'd showered and gotten dressed. I'd watched the news while I'd eaten my breakfast. I'd even listened to an audio book on my way to work.

Then I'd found myself at my office that morning, still desperately trying to get the image out of my head. I'd failed miserably, of course. So it only increased my irritation when a few hours later I stood in the man's ridiculous open-plan office, tapping my foot on the concrete floor and trying not to lose my temper as he dilly-dallied.

Finally, Jack walked over, an entourage of three of his staffers—all young women I might add—in tow. He gave me that playboy grin. "Ready?"

"Um…yes, are we all meeting?"

"I didn't say we were meeting, Candie. I said to

come down here if you wanted to know what I am up to."

Without further explanation, he headed down the stairs. The girls were right behind him. I shook my head as if this could somehow clear it and Jack would suddenly make sense. Without any other choice, I followed him.

Rather than stopping on another floor, Jack went all the way down and headed straight for the front doors. I had driven to the office that day and parked in the garage, which meant that I'd come in the back way. As a result, I had no idea a crowd of reporters had been gathering on the front steps of the building. I also had no idea volunteers were there with signs, water to pass out, and, of course, the typical protest chanting.

All noise came to an abrupt halt when Jack stepped out onto the stairs. There were maybe four dozen people out here between the reporters, photographers, volunteers, and curious homeless guys who'd stopped panhandling for a minute to watch the show.

Jack stood on the second to top step and raised his hands in welcome. A few cameras started snapping, and I woke up. I stood right behind Jack, squished between the blonde from yesterday and an even younger-looking brunette. The last thing I needed was a picture circulating of me standing there.

In my panic, I shoved myself against the brunette, nearly sending her careening off the top step and into Jack. I worked my way over to the side, then slipped down the stairway so I stood out of the way of the cameras.

"Thank you all for coming," Jack said. "I know there has been a lot of speculation about the Woolsey

Building project."

My heart started to race as my brain caught up to the scene playing out in front of me. I'd been unprepared for this in so many ways. While I'd been checking up on Jack, I hadn't spent any time looking into his projects. And there I was, being ambushed by this jerk at a press conference, and I had no idea what the hell he was talking about.

"It's true that Homes Without Inc. has taken on the Woolsey Building as our newest project. We are not afraid of Grover and Company or the DA."

Oh shit! Here I was, just days after being told by my boss that my number-one priority was to keep Jack off Grover and Company, and I watched Jack announce to the world that he was getting tougher on Grover. I was so screwed.

"Big development companies like Morrison and Grover think they can throw good, honest people out on the street just so they can make a few bucks," Jack said, speaking as if he were holding court. "But this is San Francisco. This is a town of innovation and business, yes, but it's also a town of compassion, idealism, and social justice. And we will not stand for greed, corruption, and betrayal."

I had to hand it to him. Jack Morrison was an excellent public speaker, charismatic and energetic. The crowd responded to him. His volunteers, the homeless guys, and a handful of passersby all cheered, throwing fists in the air.

A reporter stepped forward and shouted a question to Jack as the crowd died down. "Jack, the DA has publicly made you his enemy number one. He says that if you get out of line this time, he's going to prosecute.

Are you worried about ending up in jail?"

"Absolutely not," Jack said defiantly. "If we live in fear of what the corrupt machine will do, we let them win. I'll fight, from behind bars if I have to."

That's when I realized that going to jail was what Jack really wanted. He wanted a big noisy trial, a trial that would bring the focus of the entire city to his cause. Was the DA stupid enough to give Jack what he wanted?

Another reporter asked Jack a question. She was beautiful, well put together, with a smooth voice. I'd seen her on TV before. I watched her look at Jack from her place at the bottom of the steps. Her eyes and her body language said that she wanted him. Or maybe she'd already had him and she wanted more.

Perhaps there was more to Jack Morrison's good looks than just a convenience. Perhaps they were part of his toolkit.

"Jack, what about Morrison and Sons?" the reporter asked. "They've refused to press charges against you, over and over. Are you still currently targeting the Baldy Building that they own? Your brother has made it clear he won't give up his plans to remove the tenants, demolish the building, and put high-priced condos in its place. Do you think the generosity of your family is finally going to wane?"

Jack flashed his yes-I'm-sexy-as-hell grin, and winked at her. And I knew then that he'd arranged this. He'd told her to ask that question. "Well, Rory, I'm glad you asked about Morrison. Just because we're launching a new effort against Grover and Company doesn't mean we'll be taking the eye off the ball with Morrison. And no, they don't like it. As a matter of fact, they sent one of their lawyers here today to stop this press conference." He turned and pointed straight at me.

The cameras all turned, the crowd stared, and I froze. I held absolutely still, not even breathing. A long beat of silence passed before Jack called the attention back to himself.

I didn't hear him after that. Blood pounded in my ears. Sheer rage overtook me. He'd tricked me, manipulated me, and thrown me under the bus. I was going to get fired, and it was *his* fault. I'd never disliked anyone more in my life than I did Jack Morrison at that moment.

I was still wrapped up in my internal dialogue of hate and vengeance when the press conference ended. I stayed rooted to the spot as the crowd and reporters dispersed.

Jack had the nerve to walk over to me. He placed a hand on my upper arm. "Candie, would you like to come up to my office and talk now?" he asked. His voice was soft and kind.

But I didn't care how nice he pretended to be. This monstrous jackass just got me fired from my dream job. I intended to kill him.

"You know what," I said as calmly as possible, "I would like to speak somewhere in private."

Jack actually looked like he had concern in his eyes. What a lying piece of crap. He didn't care about me; he'd made that abundantly clear when he'd torpedoed me just a few moments ago.

"Are you up for a walk? There's a place we can go about three blocks away," he said.

I nodded brusquely, ripped my arm away from his

hand, and held it out to indicate he should lead the way. We didn't speak at all during our walk. He took me deeper into the heart of the bad part of the city.

Eventually, Jack stopped outside an old tenement building, probably built in the 1930s. Instead of looking decrepit and rundown, though, it looked newly renovated. The brick walls had been patched and painted. The front door was brand new.

Jack opened the door with a security code on a fancy modern lock. We walked through a charming lobby with newly laid black and white tiles and freshly painted metal mailboxes. The original pieces of this historic building were all there but had been lovingly restored.

He led me down a long hallway to a brand-new elevator. At this point, I probably should have been worried about where he was taking me, but I was too focused on my anger. All the while we moved toward our confrontation, I formulated my attack.

Jack Morrison would pay for what he'd done to me.

Chapter 4

The elevator came to a stop on the top floor, and we walked out into a dimly lit hallway. The original character of the building had been retained in the new application of elaborate and richly colored wallpaper and hardwood floors. Set into the wall in the center of the hallway was an old metal laundry chute with a wooden handle, both original, both polished and cared for.

Only two doors stood up here, one on each end of the hallway. Jack led me to the door on the right. A polished-brass number sixteen hung in the center of it. Jack opened the door and stood aside, gesturing for me to enter.

The lights were not on, but they weren't needed. This place captured every morsel of natural light available. I walked into a small foyer. The rest of the apartment spread out to my right. To access the living room, I had to walk through the bright yellow kitchen. Two large windows lit up the tidy space. No dirty dishes lay in the sink, and the pots and pans were organized on a hanging rack above the spotless island.

Giant windows kept the living room well lit. It, too, was spotless with the exception of a small pile of mail and a paperback book sitting on the coffee table. The overstuffed leather couch and the vintage easy chair called to me to sit on them. But I remained standing.

I folded my arms across my chest and glared at Jack as he moseyed into the room. "You ambushed me."

Jack came to a stop a few feet away and nodded. "I did."

"That's it?" I spread my arms out and leaned forward. My voice rose despite my effort to control it. "That's all you have to say?"

"What do you want me to say? You're smart. You can see what I did back there. I used you for my own gain."

"You're a prick!"

"I'm not surprised you feel that way. But I *am* sorry you had to get caught in the crossfire." He moved to the couch and took a seat in the middle of it, purposefully giving me the high ground.

He slung his arms over the back of the couch casually, making him look like an arrogant ass. And that is exactly what I thought of him at that moment. So I called him on his supposed apology. "Are you?"

"Yes, I am. But you're not innocent, Candie. You put yourself in this position by going to work for Morrison."

"It's Candace!" I shouted, on the edge of insanity.

He didn't respond. He just looked at me with that infuriatingly handsome face and waited, an amused look dancing on his face.

I narrowed my eyes. "John Jr!" I spat.

He laughed. My blood boiled.

I paced the room. By admitting he'd screwed me over, he'd made all the things I planned to say to him moot. So I dug down and played dirty. "I thought you respected my parents?"

"I do," he said simply.

I lost it then. My open hand pumped on my chest the way my mother's always did when she was worked up, the way my preacher grandfather's did when he was on fire at the podium. "I'm going to get fired! You don't even know me! You never even gave me a chance! You just showed up to work today and said to yourself, 'I think I'll get that woman fired.' Fuck you, Jack!"

He still wasn't reacting. In fact, he settled deeper into the couch and smiled at me. I wanted to hit something.

"I don't think you'll be fired, Candace," he said calmly. "I did a lot worse to that prick Kent, and I hear he got promoted."

I took a deep breath. Maybe he was right. Maybe I wasn't going to get fired. It still sucked, though.

Jack stood up and walked toward me. He stopped about two feet away. What a dumb move. Now he was within striking distance. "If you do get fired—which I do not think will happen—I can find you a job, a *real* job with a nonprofit that needs a lawyer. Hell..." He shrugged. "I might hire you myself. I could use a lawyer that's passed the bar. I've got two pre-law students and a former legal aid. They're great, but they could use more guidance."

I stared at him, my mouth agape. This guy was a piece of work.

"Candace," he said placing his hands on my upper arms and looking me in the eye, which, despite my heels, involved him stooping a little since I refused to look up at him. "I am certain, come tomorrow morning, you will still be working at Morrison, and I will still be

35

your assigned project. And I promise I will meet with you next week."

Dazed, I repeated weakly, "Next week?"

"Yes, I'm leaving a day early to go out of town for the weekend. But first thing Monday morning, we'll sit down, and I will tell you what I'm up to."

I wanted to believe him. God help me, I did. But I had to remember I was playing with fire here. This man was a master. I had to stay on my toes.

I wrenched myself away from him, took a couple steps back, and spat out, "We'll see. If I'm lucky, I'll get fired, and I won't have to deal with you anymore."

This made him laugh. Which made my blood boil. So I stormed out of the apartment and made it to the elevator before he had time to get in there with me. Back on the street, I hailed a cab and made the cabbie drive me the three short blocks back to Jack's office building so I could retrieve my car. I gave the guy a twenty-dollar tip.

****

Normally, Thursday nights were my favorite nights of the week. I taught an adult-education class. The course helped everyday people navigate the legal system and covered everything from wills to divorce to bail bonds and arraignments.

But I was so out of sorts that day because of Jack that I couldn't lecture. Instead, I put on a movie about probate courts and sat in the back of the classroom wallowing in self-pity. It was not my finest moment.

After class, I headed home. I lived in the East Bay, and I liked it there. First of all, because it was cheaper, I could get a nicer place. I had the entire second floor of a remodeled Victorian in Berkeley for the price of a tiny studio in San Francisco.

Living across the bay also gave me an excuse sometimes not to do things I didn't want to with my parents. I know that sounds awful, but I'm not talking about ditching out on them for dinner or a family gathering. I'm talking about things that ended with handcuffs.

My parents were always trying to get me to participate in crazy events with their activist friends. Some were tame music festivals, but other times they were the kind of "event" where people ended up chained to a bulldozer or with their mug shot on the news, and I just didn't need it. So I would say, "Oh, Dad, you know how the bridge can be on Saturday morning. I just can't get there in time." Or "Oh, Mom, I have an appointment in the East Bay, so there's no way I can get over to you and back again in time." I knew it was cowardly, but, hey, it was survival.

That night, as I collapsed onto my couch and stared at my six tropical fish swimming dozily in their thirty-gallon tank, I managed to keep myself from crying. I tended to be an easy crier so I considered this a major feat. Frustration usually started my tears. I could control them in public, but as soon as I got home, they would spill out.

Letting my tears flow usually released my tension. But I wouldn't do it that night. I refused to let Jack freaking Morrison make me cry. Instead, I reordered my thinking. Jack was put in front of me as a challenge. He was the mountain I had to climb to get what I wanted. Assuming I still had a job tomorrow, I would have a choice to make. I could accept the challenge and find a way to deal with Jack, using the same amount of guile and deceit on him that he'd used on me, or I could give up.

I had spent too many years, too much money, and too much dreaming, to give up on my personal goals. This job might have been horrible, but I considered it a first step to the career I'd always wanted. And despite my flaws, namely my easy frustration, I was the fighter my parents had raised. And I intended to fight for my future.

So I decided, if I still had a job in the morning, I would climb the mountain. I would take on the challenge of this ridiculous assignment with gusto. Look out, Jack Morrison!

****

Friday morning came, and I couldn't seem to control my fear. I had trouble deciding what to wear. What did one wear to their own firing? In the end, I picked a professional, but low-cut, blouse and a sharp pencil skirt. Sexy and in command, the ultimate woman, that's how I was going to look for my firing.

After I'd dressed, I decided driving to work was definitely a better idea than taking BART. After all, who wanted to wait at the train station holding back tears after being fired? I also decided to take a very large purse rather than an extra bag. If I got fired, I would just shove all my stuff in there rather than admit defeat ahead of time by walking in with an extra bag, telling all the world I knew exactly what was going to happen.

I walked in on my four-inch heels with my head held high. My shoulder-length hair hung down, perfectly styled with just the right amount of bounce and curl. My blouse clung to me in all the right places without looking trashy. I marched through the lobby, throwing pleasant greetings to each person I came across.

Relief washed over me. I would be able to drop the act for a moment when I reached the safety of my own office. But, as I breezed through the doorway, my breath hitched in my throat.

Sitting in my chair, with his feet propped up on my desk, was Hayden Morrison.

"Good morning, Candace," he said, his playboy grin in full force. He moved his feet off my desk and sat up in the chair.

I stood frozen in front of him, which gave him a chance to look me up and down slowly. Good, get a good look so you're sorry when you fire me.

I dropped my giant purse and my briefcase on the desk and stuck a hand on my cocked hip. "Good morning, Hayden." Ha! No "Mr. Morrison" for you. You won't make me crawl.

"Please, have a seat," he said, gesturing to the guest chair I kept opposite my desk.

Damn it. This was bad. Hayden sat at *my* desk, with me across from him. He wielded power over me, and I hated it.

"I'd rather stand," I said forcefully.

He grinned at me. Dimples peeked out, just like on his stupid brother. "Okay, well, first of all, about Jack—" he began.

"Look, Hayden," I interrupted. "He got the better of me yesterday. He won. I realize this." I changed my stance so my arms were folded over my chest. "You don't need to drag this out. Am I fired?"

Hayden's eyes got big. He stood up. "No, hell no!"

He came around the desk so that we stood a few feet apart. "God no! I just wanted to give you a little comfort is all. I know my brother is a pain in the ass. That shit he pulled with you yesterday, that's pretty much par for the course. Kent got it way worse."

So Jack hadn't been exaggerating. Interesting. The good news had my shoulders relaxing.

Hayden ran a hand through his hair. He appeared to have an imitation of Jack's messy do, but he wasn't quite pulling it off the same. He chuckled and the low, casual tone of it struck me. "I remember he even got a restraining order against Kent once. He told the cops Kent was his ex-lover who'd threatened to kill him. It took us a while to sort that out."

I would have laughed if I hadn't been so busy worrying right up to that very moment. My arms involuntarily dropped to my sides. "Really?"

"Yeah, what he pulled yesterday was pretty tame. Don't worry about it." Hayden reached out and put a hand on my shoulder. "You'll do fine with Jack. He's manipulative and conniving, but you're way smarter." He winked at me. "Better?"

I felt a little like a child being comforted. And I didn't like it. "Well, if that's the case, I will do better with my assignment in the future," I said stiffly.

Hayden's hand remained on my shoulder and now his thumb rubbed back and forth. "The real reason I came down here was to ask if you would have lunch with me today."

Whoa. The boss just asked me out! This was definitely dicey territory here.

"I would be happy to go to a business-based lunch with you, Hayden," I said, trying to assert my professionalism.

He smiled and dropped his hand from my shoulder. "I know what you're thinking. But don't be alarmed, Candace. I'm not your boss, you know."

"My boss's boss," I suggested.

"Not really. I think we both know I don't wield any real power at Morrison and Sons."

I smiled at him. "I'd be happy to go to a business lunch with you, Hayden."

I was too smart to screw up my career by dating him. But I *did* like him, and what was the harm in spending time with someone more like me than the Che Guevara wannabes my mother was always setting me up with? Plus, I could drill him about how to handle his pain-in-the-ass brother.

"I'll come get you at one, then," he said, flashing that playboy grin again as he walked out the door.

I moved around my desk and slumped into my seat. I was relieved I hadn't been fired, a little disappointed I hadn't been taken off my current assignment, and definitely confused about Hayden asking me out.

The Morrison brothers were sure making my life interesting.

****

Twenty minutes later, Janice buzzed me. "Ms. Gleason, Jack Morrison is on the phone for you."

I'd just started reading the file about the Baldy building and the media battle Hayden and Jack were having over it. I minimized the document on my computer and hit the speaker button on my phone.

"Candace Gleason," I said as politely as I could.

"Hi, Candace."

"What can I do for you, Mr. Morrison?"

"Mr. Morrison? No one calls me that, ever."

I sighed. "What do you want, Jack?"

"That's better." I could hear him grin right over the phone. "I just called to see if you still have a job."

"I do. Does that disappoint you?"

He chuckled. "No. Not at all. Believe it or not, Candace, I *am* looking forward to working with you. You have the genes and the upbringing to make a good activist. I'm hoping to foster the inclination."

So I was to be his project, just as he was mine.

"As you well know, Jack, a person's birthright does not determine their path in life."

"Touché," he said.

"I thought you were out of town."

"I am. I'm at a conference in New York right now, as a matter of fact."

"A *conference*," I said sarcastically. "Is that what you call your hippie gatherings to make it sound more professional?"

"You know, Candace, there's more to running an organization than protests and press conferences. There's staffing, fundraising, legal issues. At this conference, I'm learning how to set up an endowment to secure the organization's financial future. This isn't some pet project of mine," he said angrily.

I thought about being contrite. But I was still plenty pissed at Jack, so instead I said, "Okay, well, try not to get arrested."

He let out a long sigh. "I'm glad you didn't get fired. I'll see you next week." And then he hung up.

I started to feel bad, for just a fraction of a second. Then, I remembered who I was dealing with. Right that moment, Jack was probably getting ready to tie himself to a backhoe somewhere, and I was the last person he wanted to tell about it. Conference in New York, as if.

Chapter 5

Hayden took me to a hot new restaurant for lunch. I had been dying to go there since it opened two months before. If you didn't have reservations that had been made while they were still pouring the concrete, or if you weren't "somebody," forget even getting a foot in the door. Hayden *was* somebody, and we got a great table right away.

The food was fantastic, even if the small portions were bound to leave me hungry and munching on cheesy puffs in my office an hour later. The place had incredible atmosphere. The dimmed lights, funky decorations, and soft din of the crowd had me sitting up straighter, holding my chin higher. I felt important. I felt like a diva.

Hayden was good company, charming and funny. I listened intently as he told me stories about growing up in the Morrison mansion. I hung on his every word as he talked about family trips to Europe, spring breaks in Mexico, and Caribbean cruises with his mom. When I asked him about missing school for all these vacations, he just shrugged and said they had private tutors. He told me stories about Jack and Chelsea, too.

"Jack was fun when we were kids," he said, leaning back in his chair.

Half a dozen tiny plates littered the table in front of us, all of them empty. We were just talking now, ignoring the clock.

I had initially been worried about getting back to the office. When Hayden's attempts to get me to relax weren't successful, he'd called Tom Garrity and told him that I was out with him. I didn't like the special treatment. A niggling feeling of discomfort stayed with me until we started talking about Jack. That felt more like recon and, therefore, work. So I sipped on a raspberry lemonade while Hayden drank a White Russian and told me about his childhood years with Jack.

"We're less than three years apart, so we were each other's playmates. Of course, that also made our fights all the more intense." He flashed his dimples at me. "I remember one time at school. God, I think Jack was in sixth grade, and I was in fourth." He waved his hand. "Something like that. Anyway, Jack had put a stink bomb in the girls' bathroom." He laughed. "And then the asshole blamed it on me." He shook his head. "I was so pissed. We got into a fight right there in the headmaster's office." He laughed again. "Scared the crap out of that poor bastard. It was twelve hours until my mother showed up, and we were 'sequestered' in this room together all that time. After we beat the shit out of each other some more, we figured out the room had a vent in it. So we climbed into the damn thing and shimmied through the air duct. God, we were little then. Anyway, it went to the girls' locker room." Hayden put his hands behinds his head, lacing his fingers together. "Life didn't get any better than that."

"So this was boarding school?" I asked, fascinated by the idea of anything other than the public schools I'd spent all my formal education in.

"Yeah, and by the time my mom flew there to get us, we were getting along again just fine. But we still got suspended for a week. So she had to take us home."

"What about Chelsea?" I asked. "What was she like as a kid?" I wasn't intentionally taking the focus off Jack. But as an only child, I'd always wanted to know everything I could about what it was like to have siblings. And the Morrison siblings were more interesting than most.

"Ah, Chelsea. She and I didn't get along. When she showed up, I was four and jealous as hell. Jack was almost seven and had a completely different take on it. He doted on Chelsea. Between him and my dad, you'd think she was the crown princess or something." He made the statement lightly, but obviously there was more to it.

"She's in college now, right?"

"Yeah, Stanford, of course. Following in Jack's footsteps, majoring in business. Hopefully, she won't drop out like he did."

"What about you, Hayden?" I asked, wanting to make him feel he had my attention and I wasn't just interested in hearing about his siblings. "What were your college days like?"

He grinned and his eyes lit up. I could tell he liked this topic much better. "One giant party. I went to FSU and majored in Liberal Arts. What about you?"

"I worked my ass off." I shrugged casually. "Got a scholarship for undergraduate at the University of San Francisco, then went to law school at Pepperdine. I don't remember a lot of partying."

Hayden leaned forward. "You seem like a very serious woman, Candace."

"I am," I admitted.

"So what do you do for fun?"

What a good question. What *did* I do for fun? I'd spent seven years studying my ass off. When I wasn't studying, I was interning at high-level law firms. I did occasionally go out with Grace. She'd taken me to some very cool places. And I liked to go camping with my parents in Yosemite, but I would never admit that.

"I go out, you know. I do some traveling, too." Sure, when Grace and Eric were paying.

"Yeah, where've you been?"

"Let's see," I said, biting my lip as if the list was so long I had to choose. "Berlin." Where Eric had been stationed two years ago. "Barcelona." Where Eric was last year. "Places like that. If I want to stay closer to home, I go to Baja or Hawaii." The former being where Grace and her parents took me one spring break, and the latter being where Grace and Eric got married.

"Well traveled, smart, *and* sexy. You are the whole package, Candace." Rather than sounding sleazy, the way he said it was flattering, and it made me blush. I'm pretty sure men like Hayden were taught how to deliver a line like that and make a woman melt when they were still in diapers.

But he couldn't play me that easily. "You are still basically my boss," I warned him.

He leaned over the table, getting as close to me as he could. Then he reached his hand out and placed it over mine. "You worry too much, Candace. I told you, I'm a nobody. My sister is the future CEO of this company. But I will always have a consolation prize job and a secure future."

Meg, my closest girlfriend all through college at

USF, would be throwing up right now. When she lifted her head, she'd scream at me to run away from this arrogant, rich boy. But I wasn't running. I was buying it all.

Hayden's eyes pierced me. One lock of hair flopped over his forehead. One dimple gleamed at me. My lips parted. My breath grew shorter, into little pants. And Hayden, who had no doubt been reading the signs from women since grade school, pounced. "Have dinner with me tomorrow night, Candace."

This was stupid. So stupid.

"Sure," I breathed.

****

Dinner with the boss's son at what I was sure would be an exclusive restaurant took a lot of wardrobe planning. But with Grace MIA, I had to ask Meg to help me. And that turned out to be a huge mistake.

"I'm telling you, Candace, you should put a stop to this right now," she lectured as I pulled things out of my closet and laid them out on the bed.

I looked at her. Meg was one of those women who exuded self-confidence. She wore no makeup because her natural beauty made it wholly unnecessary. She wore the clothes she wanted to, regardless of fashion standards, because everything looked good on her. But she dated total losers. The men Meg ended up with treated her like crap, and they were usually unemployed, or artists, or worked in a record store somewhere. She usually paid for dates and occasionally even gave her boyfriends loans to keep them from becoming homeless.

"Look, Meg, you need to set aside your prejudice against rich guys for a minute."

"I am *not* prejudiced against rich guys." She had the nerve to look affronted.

"Bullshit," I said, tossing down my most expensive evening gown and turning to glare at her.

Meg came from a family like mine, middle class, not destitute, but not wealthy either. But unlike me, Meg had no desire to rise above her economic station. She was perfectly happy just squeaking by each month and having a roommate.

"Look, it's just that I know firsthand what they can be like," she said.

Here we go. Meg had dated one rich guy in high school, actually *all through* high school. And his parents wanted him to marry some friend of the family they'd picked out for him. So, on the eve of graduation he'd dumped her. She'd never forgotten, or forgiven.

"Meg," I said, touching her arm. "I'm not planning to marry the guy. It's just dinner."

She stared at me, one eyebrow raised, assessing the situation. "Okay, but he's your boss or whatever. I know you, Candace, and that kind of thing is way outside your comfort zone. You are straight and narrow. Especially when it comes to your career. Remember when I tried to get you to try pot? You threw a fit because you were worried that if you were ever up for the Supreme Court it would come up during the congressional hearings."

"I told you, he's not really my boss."

"So he says."

I pulled the last of my dresses out of the closet and laid it on the bed with the rest, then I turned to her, hands on my hips. "Would it make you feel better if I asked my actual boss about it?"

"You gonna do that?"

"I already did."

"Seriously?" Her eyes popped open. "You are so bizarre, Candace. Who does that?"

"I do. Because, like you said, my career is too important to me to jeopardize."

"And? What did your boss say? No, wait. First, tell me how the hell you asked a question like that."

"I just said Hayden had asked me out and I wanted to know if it would be appropriate to accept. Tom said as long I didn't feel pressured to go out with Hayden—"

"AKA sexual harassment."

"Yes, exactly. Tom said interoffice dating wasn't against any policies at Morrison. Furthermore, he told me Hayden didn't oversee the legal department, and he didn't see a conflict at all. To be honest, he kind of seemed happy about it."

"Weird...and a little creepy."

I rolled my eyes. "The bottom line is, there is no ethical dilemma. The guy is charming, nice, rich, and hot. So help me pick out something to wear, please."

"Tell me more about his brother."

"His brother is a pain in the ass."

"But is he also charming, nice, rich, and hot?"

"He's not charming. He's irritating. And he's not rich because he sinks all his family money into his nonprofit. And he's not nice either. He ambushed me."

"Hmmm. I noticed you didn't address whether or not he is hot."

I rolled my eyes and gestured to the pile of clothes. "Meg, please, I'm begging you. What should I wear?"

She sighed and walked over to my bed. Then—and

this was why I'd called her in the first place—she plucked an absolutely perfect maroon cocktail dress out of the pile and held it up.

"Wear this," she said lifelessly.

****

"Un-be-lieve-able!" I told Janice. "This cannot be happening."

"I have a flight booked for you. It leaves in ninety minutes. If you drive straight to the airport, you should be able to make—"

"Janice, do you realize I am on a date?" I hissed into the phone.

My date sat in our private booth at the high-priced restaurant while I stood at the front desk talking on their phone. I still have no idea how Janice managed to track me down since I had turned off my cell, and I didn't tell her where I'd be.

"I'm so sorry, Ms. Gleason, but Mr. Garrity said it was imperative you get to New York right away."

"Great," I mumbled.

The head of the legal department wanted something done, and it was going to get done. Forget that it was eight o'clock on a Saturday night or that I was on a date with the boss's son.

"Okay, text me the info, and I'll get to the airport." I hung up and walked back to our booth.

Hayden and I had just arrived when the hostess came to get me for the phone call. We hadn't even decided on the wine yet. Hayden sat there anticipating me. He looked good in his fitted black slacks, crisp white shirt with no tie, and an open navy blazer.

"I'm sorry," I said. I grabbed my purse and stood in front of him.

He slid out and stood, too. "You're leaving?"

Hayden was a good three inches shorter than his brother, and with my heels on I almost looked him in the eye. I liked that about him. And right at that moment, everything about him seemed better than Jack.

"Your brother," I said.

He rolled his eyes. "What did he do this time?"

"Apparently, he's sitting in a jail cell in New York. Garrity and your dad made arrangements to get him out with no charges pressed, but they want me to go pick him up and bring him home."

"So you have to leave our date to go babysit my big brother."

"Yep."

"That figures. Let me take you to the airport."

Chapter 6

At eight months old, I had been strapped to my mother's chest when she managed to get arrested at a rally in front of City Hall. I spent a few hours in the police station while my father made his way through the traffic to get me and through the red tape to get her. Aside from that experience, of which I have no memory, I'd never been in a police station until I met Jack freaking Morrison.

Getting him out wasn't hard at all. In fact, they were waiting for me to show up. I think the cops wanted to get him off their hands. Pissed that his dad had pulled strings, Jack yelled and carried on as they brought him out to me.

"I should be staying here! You got bought off, you fat cats!" he shouted as they ushered him into the lobby.

"Get him out of here," one cop said as he shoved Jack toward me.

Jack managed to stop his ranting and raving for a minute and look at me. For a split second, I thought he was going to calm down. I was wrong.

He whirled back around. "This is bullshit!"

"Get the hell out of here, or I'll arrest *her*!" the cop said, pointing at me.

What the hell did I do? I stood there like a deer in headlights. Holy shit, was Jack freaking Morrison about to get me arrested?

"Fine, assholes!" Jack turned on his heel, grabbed my arm, and pulled me out of the police station.

This man was completely ruining my life. My anger left me speechless. To keep myself from expressing how very pissed off I was, I simply followed him for a while in silence. He walked out to the street and hailed a cab. Moving stiffly, I got into the cab with him.

"Take me to the Excellent Eleven hotel on sixth," Jack told the cabbie.

Finally, I found my voice. "What the hell, Jack?" I blurted out.

He turned to me. "Nice to see you, Candie."

The jerk was perfectly relaxed. He leaned back in the seat, stretching his legs as far as possible in the back of the cab. He tucked his hands behind his head and took a couple of deep breaths. What could almost pass for a smile played on his lips.

I lost it. "Jack Morrison, you are at the very top of my shit list!"

"I'm sure I am, but keep in mind this is really all your fault," he said casually.

I had to pick my jaw up off the floor. "Excuse me?"

"Candie," he said, turning toward me. "You set the expectation for me. I was just hanging out at a boring conference about fundraising. But you told me what you expected of me. 'Don't get arrested, Jack,' you said. And I got to thinking. I've been living down to the low expectations of my family for years now. Why shouldn't I let you down, too?"

"There is something seriously wrong with you."

He had the nerve to grin. "Look," he said, a serious

tone suddenly taking over him. He pulled his hands out from behind his head and sat up straighter, angling toward me. "I met some people at the conference, and we became friends."

I just bet it was that easy for him. I had exactly two friends in the whole world, and this guy, he could make a dozen in the course of two days.

"They were holding a demonstration downtown," he continued, "to bring attention to the plight of women being trafficked and to shed light on the lack of anything real being done about it by the authorities. Surely you care about human trafficking, Candie."

I did care. I cared a lot. In fact, I donated money to groups like that every year, and I volunteered my time. I wondered if Jack had somehow figured that out. But I didn't answer him. I kept my expression neutral as I returned his stare.

"It was a peaceful demonstration. We weren't doing anything wrong," he told me, a sincere look on his face.

That was one of many problems with Jack—he excelled at looking sincere. I pierced him with my skeptical glare.

"I swear." He held up his hands. "The cops got rough, and things got out of hand. And, Candie, I got out of jail while my friends are still sitting there. Can you see how that would piss me off? Can you imagine how that would feel?"

I struggled to respond. What could I say? Should I express my anger that my date had been interrupted or that I'd had to fly out here on a Saturday night? It fell flat against his argument.

"What are you going to do?" I asked, my voice

soft.

"Unfortunately, there isn't a lot I can do. All my lawyer connections are in California. And I don't suppose you have a license to practice in New York." He sounded defeated.

"I could call my dad. He knows people in New York." What the hell was I doing? It had just popped out of my mouth. I didn't usually speak before thinking. But for some reason, Jack freaking Morrison made me completely lose my mind.

Jack's eyes lit up at my outburst. "Oh God, Candie, really? Thank you!" I was still reeling from what I'd done when the taxi pulled up to a curb and Jack took my hand, pulling me out of the car. "Come on, we can call him from my room."

I looked up in dismay at the Excellent Eleven. It hadn't been a sick joke. This man's trust fund provided enough money to stay in the Ritz, and he had dragged me to a fifty-nine-dollar-a-night motel.

I stopped on the sidewalk, looking up at the neon sign. "Are you serious?"

"As a heart attack. It's clean, and the walls aren't too thin. I'm a big fan. Come on." He tugged on my elbow.

Reluctantly, I followed him up a set of metal stairs. This definitely broke Grace's rule of never staying in a hotel where your room had to be accessed from the outside. He came to a stop in front of a green door with the number 226 hanging crookedly above the peephole. He used the key card and held the door open for me as if he were ushering me into anywhere better than an Excellent Eleven.

Jack flicked on the light, and I looked around. It

wasn't that bad. In fact, my parents and I had stayed in similar hotels on our travels many times. It's just I'd made a pact with myself never to set foot in one again now that I had the six-figure salary of a corporate lawyer.

Jack settled me into a chair at the tiny square table shoved into one corner of the room. Then he went to the vanity and used the mini-coffee maker to brew us both a hot cup of joe.

Jack placed the Styrofoam cup in front of me. "Black, right?"

"Actually, I like cream." I told him. "But they probably only have that powdered stuff here." I wrinkled my nose.

Jack chuckled. "Unfortunately, yes. You want it?"

I shook my head, and Jack took a seat across from me. He looked at me over the rim of his cup as he took a sip. "You are never what I expect you to be, Candie."

"What the hell does that mean?" I asked without much gusto. I was tired of trying to figure Jack out at the moment. But I didn't want to let that go either.

He shrugged. "You just constantly surprise me, that's all. One minute you're offering to help me out, the next you're all high-maintenance about the hotel and your coffee."

I took a sip of my coffee. It didn't taste nearly as bad as I'd expected. I also wasn't angry at Jack's statement as I might have expected to be. I liked that I made Jack's head spin as much as he made mine.

When I didn't respond to him, he smiled at me and leaned over the table, propped on his elbows. "So, you ready to call your dad?"

I sighed but pulled my phone out and set it on the

table between us. I hit the speaker button, and then I dialed.

****

My dad was delighted to help out. He might have jumped through the phone to hug us both if he could. As it turned out, he did know someone in New York who could help. My dad hung up to make a few calls and told us he'd check in with us in about an hour.

The story Jack told my father about the arrest really bothered me. According to Jack, the leader of the local organization that arranged the demonstration was a woman named Joyce. He'd met her at the conference. An open lesbian, Joyce had been in a relationship with the arresting officer's sister the year before. The sister had been closeted up until then, and the officer had expressed vitriol over his sister's sexuality. He blamed Joyce. Even after the relationship ended, the officer harassed Joyce. Jack contended this was the sole reason behind the arrest.

Despite my parents' rhetoric, I had always believed in the basic infallibility of the American justice system. But, if what Jack told my father was true, and three people sat in jail on trumped-up charges over homophobia—well, it was messing with my head.

"Hungry?" Jack asked me after I tucked the phone back into my purse.

It was eight o'clock in the morning. I hadn't slept at all on the plane. I sat in a cheap motel three thousand miles from home helping Jack get some hippies out of jail. Of course, I was hungry.

"Starving," I told him.

"There is a great restaurant around the corner. They have amazing french toast."

"There isn't enough good french toast in the world."

"Agreed," he replied, getting up.

I stood, too. Jack looked me over. "Man, I would go to jail everyday if I knew you were going to show up looking like that to bail me out."

I had completely forgotten I still wore the cocktail dress and heels from last night. "I was on a date."

"Really? Tell me about it over breakfast," he said, opening the door.

I most certainly did not want to tell him about my date. And I fumed over it as we walked to the restaurant.

"How do you walk in those things?" Jack asked, eyeing my heels as we headed up the steps to the entrance of the restaurant.

"It's a gift," I said, blowing by him as he held the door for me.

The coffee here was even better than the stuff Jack made at the hotel. Once we had steaming mugs nestled in our hands and we'd each ordered a giant stack of french toast, I thought I'd give Jack a hard time. "I suppose I need to pay for this out of my per diem."

Jack didn't laugh. "No. And quit trying to deflect. Tell me about your date that I interrupted."

"Why on earth would you care?"

"You're my babysitter. I want to know more about you."

I laughed. "You know I tried to find a way not to call myself that the first time we met."

He grinned. "I'm sure you did."

I had absolutely no idea why I was sitting in a diner having easy conversation with my archnemesis. But I hadn't slept in about twenty-five hours, and I was stuck here with him until our flight back this afternoon. So what harm would it do to get to know each other better? In fact, I might do better with him if I gave a little.

However, I had no intention of revealing I had been on a date with his brother. "How about this, you can ask me about anything *other* than my date," I proposed.

"Okay," he said, rubbing his hands together. "Tell me what it was like to grow up being you?"

"Whoa, that's pretty broad."

"So?"

"So, I'm not a good storyteller. I can't just tell you what it was like to be me. You need to ask me more directed questions."

"Okay, you're an only child, right?"

I nodded.

"What was that like?"

"Jealous?" I ribbed.

"Maybe. Though I'm not sure I'd trade Chelsea in."

"You wanna tell me about you and your brother?"

"No, I want to talk about you."

I shrugged. "What is there to say? I didn't have anyone to play with, so I ended up alone a lot. I read a lot. I'm introverted. My parents were attentive, don't get me wrong. In fact, they were too attentive." I laughed.

"Did they put a lot of pressure on you?"

"I guess. No different from any other kid with loving parents who want to mold and shape them into their own image."

"I can relate."

"I bet. Is that why you rebelled so deeply? Because your dad wanted you to follow in his footsteps? Did he put a lot of pressure on you?" I asked, suddenly desperate to get the skinny on what exactly had happened between Jack and his family.

He scowled. "Please, don't chalk this up to rebellion. It makes it sound so trite."

"What is it then, Jack? Why do you want to destroy your family's company?"

"I don't want to destroy it. Who told you that?" Anger dripped from his voice. I was taken aback. This seemed to be a given to me. And, of course, it was the assumption of everyone I worked with.

"I don't know if a particular person told me, per se," I hedged.

"It sure as hell wasn't my father or my uncle. They know better. Hayden does too, though I wouldn't be surprised if he ran around spewing bullshit like that. I bet it was Garrity. That prick hates me."

I leaned over the table, fully invested in the conversation. Jack seemed completely put out by the idea that he was trying to sabotage his family's company. But I could see no other way to look at it. "If you aren't out to destroy the company, what is your goal, Jack?"

"To change it." He leaned forward as well, and we were bent toward one another like conspirators. "Take for example that building I live in."

"The one we were at on Thursday?"

He nodded. "That building was my first battle with Morrison. They planned to evict everyone, tear it down, and build a luxury short-term apartment building. There are people who've lived in that building since the end of the Second World War. It's a beautiful building with good units. It just needed a little love and care. I convinced my father to renovate it instead of tearing it down, keep the current tenants, and attract new tenants as units opened, charging them a slightly higher rent. And it worked. The building makes a nice little profit."

"How did you talk him into it?"

"I moved into an empty apartment, the one I live in now, as a matter of fact, and I refused to leave. Stared down the bulldozers, so to speak."

"What did your dad do?"

"He gave me the building."

"What?"

"He literally gave it to me. Said if I could show him my idea, rather than tell it, he'd be willing to talk about future projects."

"And?" I asked, leaning over even farther.

Jack and I were just inches away from each other now. And, of course, that's when the waitress came. We both sat back as she set our plates in front of us. He dug into his pile of toast immediately.

But I held off on attacking my breakfast until I'd asked one more question. "So, have you proven yourself to your dad?"

Jack chewed on that a minute, literally and figuratively. I dug into my own breakfast, expecting a well-thought-out answer. Instead, I got "Kind of. I will."

"What does that mean?"

Jack set down his fork and looked at me. "I would have made more money by now, but I keep sinking the profits back into building renovations. I think I have it in good shape now, though. Over the next two years,

I'll have my point made and wrapped up in a bow. My dad acknowledges it. But that little building on the edge of the Tenderloin is one thing. A project like Baldy is something else entirely."

I knew what this was all about now. I'd done my research after the ill-fated press conference. The Baldy building sat on a piece of prime real estate in the SOMA district. It had originally been a Chinese laundry, but it burned to the ground in the massive fires that followed the 1906 earthquake. The owner sold the plot of land to Morton Baldy and moved east, away from the San Andreas fault. Morton Baldy had built a high-end apartment building. It catered to well-to-do families that were hesitant to rebuild after losing their homes in the great quake. Instead, they chose to rent large, luxury apartments.

Since then, it had become home to generations of San Franciscans who couldn't afford the newer apartment complexes but still wanted to live in the city. Beautiful and well cared for, it was too old and its units too outdated to be a candidate for high-rent payers. It had not been profitable for the owners Morrison and Sons purchased it from for several years. Using a loophole in California law, the new owners would soon be able to legally evict the tenants.

Hayden had taken on this building as his first project with the company. Hayden intended to evict everyone when the wait time expired in just a few weeks. Then, he planned to tear down the building and erect a brand new high-end condo complex. In the current market in San Francisco, he could sell each condo for millions. The company would make a killing.

And all that stood in Hayden's way was his big

brother.

"What do you think they should do with Baldy?" I asked, before digging back into my french toast. I almost moaned in response to the heavenly flavor.

Jack ate a little more himself before answering. "Same thing I did with the building I live in. It's historic. It should be fixed up and used as is. I have a petition in to make it a historic landmark."

I knew about this, too. If Jack succeeded, Hayden would not be able to tear down the building. "Why spend the money to fix it up and let people live there for peanuts? It just doesn't make economic sense, Jack."

Jack looked at me long and hard. I paused and stared back at him. Finally, he said, "Why don't we table this conversation and pick it up later?" Jack finished his breakfast with a few last bites, then slid his plate away and leaned back in the booth. "So, tell me about this date."

Chapter 7

"No way, Jack, we have a flight at two o'clock," I whined.

"Sorry, Candie. We're not going to make it." He looked at his watch. "We need to be in Manhattan in three hours. I feel like a nap, how about you?"

I gritted my teeth. Mr. Congenial Conversation had left. Mr. Irritating as Hell was back. I blamed my father for this as well. But, ultimately, that meant the blame fell on me because I was the one who'd involved my father.

He had contacted an attorney who agreed to meet with us at one o'clock in his office. Which meant there was no way we'd make our flight. I reluctantly called Janice. When I got off the phone, I turned around to see Jack lying on one of the two queen beds in the hotel room, eyes closed. My breath hitched as I took in his shirtless torso.

Oh, dear God. He was beautiful. It all added up: broad chest the perfect balance of muscle and smoothness with a little sprinkle of light-colored hair dusting the center, biceps just large enough to be sexy but not so large as to indicate a ridiculous amount of time wasted at the gym, and an adorable farmers' tan that came from real time outdoors.

"Jack, our new flight is at eight," I told him.

"Hmm," he murmured, eyes still closed. "Turn off

the light, and take a nap, Candie."

I stared at the other bed. My exhaustion called to me. I knew I should do something else, anything else. Maybe I should call Tom Garrity. I'd sent him a text saying I'd retrieved Jack from lock-up, but I hadn't actually given him an update. Maybe I should check my email. But it was Sunday. Other than Janice, who I'd disturbed at home, no one else would be around.

So, with nothing better to do, I gave up and lay down on the bed. It was surprisingly comfortable, and I needed sleep desperately. So I tried to forget Jack Morrison was lying in another bed, half clothed, just a few feet away. Which, of course, brought back, in vivid Technicolor, that stupid dream I'd had of Jack and me in bed.

"Damn it," I whispered as I rolled over on my side facing away from Jack. I tried to push the image from the dream I'd had about Jack last week, the dream where we were in bed together, out of my head. The harder I tried, the worse it got. So, I found myself holding completely still, every muscle in my body tensed. I tried to force my mind to behave and my body to fall into the sleep it desperately needed. I listened, hard, and the sound of Jack's deep breaths reached my ears.

In that moment, I could have obsessed over what it meant to lie so close to him, I could hear his lungs moving air in and out. Or I could have worried about why I was so in tune to the sound of him breathing deeply as he slept. But I didn't. Instead, I fell asleep within minutes.

****

I woke when the bed moved. Startled, I opened my

eyes to see Jack, still shirtless, sitting on the edge of my bed, staring down at me. "Wake up, sleepyhead. We have to catch a cab if we want to make it to our meeting in time."

I rubbed my eyes and sat up. Then I made the mistake of looking down at myself. The cocktail dress was hopelessly wrinkled. Worse, I'd been sleeping on top of the covers and the dress had ridden up on my legs to way past decent, exposing quite a bit of myself to Jack.

Jack still sat on the edge of my bed, sipping on yet more coffee. He didn't appear to notice the obscene amount of leg I was showing. Of course, that didn't mean he wasn't paying attention *before* he woke me.

I hopped off the bed so I could pull the dress down as far as humanly possible. "This is ridiculous. I need clothes."

"Are you fast?" Jack asked.

"What?"

"Can you walk into a store, find an outfit, buy it, put it on in the dressing room, and walk back out in twenty minutes or less?"

"Yes," I said honestly. "I can do that." I was an excellent shopper. It was practically a competitive sport for me.

"Good, then we'll stop somewhere on the way."

****

When we pulled up to the skyscraper that housed the offices of Hausen and Newbaker Attorneys at Law, I was wearing a very comfortable, but still flattering, pair of light purple slacks and an off-white silk button-up blouse. At Jack's behest, I had also traded my four-inch heels for a pair of ballet-slipper flats. I had to admit, that in addition to the nap, the new outfit had helped me relax.

Jack had cleaned up a bit, too. He looked more presentable than usual in a crisp white shirt and a pair of khakis, which surprised the hell out of me because I didn't think Jack even owned a pair of pants that weren't jeans. Much to my chagrin, he'd ruined the entire ensemble with boat shoes. The man was hopeless.

An eerie quiet greeted us when we arrived. Given that Sunday afternoon wasn't the peak time for business at a law firm we did not have to wait long before being ushered into the office of Richard McCrae. Richard was a middle-aged man with a classic haircut, graying at his temples. He wore a suit and tie appropriate to his high-end law firm. This was the kind of place I would want to work. Which made it all the more bizarre that *we* were here.

"Robert Gleason's daughter, I presume," he said as we shook hands.

"Nice to meet you," I responded.

"And you must be Jack Morrison. I've heard about you," he said, as he took Jack's hand. This surprised me. I didn't realize Jack's fame had followed him all the way across the country.

Richard settled us into fancy leather chairs opposite his mahogany desk. "I do my pro-bono work for LGBTQ cases," he said. "Rob gave me some background on what's going on here. Are they still being held?" he asked Jack.

"Yes. There are three of them. Though, only Joyce Constein is a member of the LGBTQ community. The other two are Tim Fisher and Cory Hellman. The four of us were part of a group of about two dozen people conducting a permitted demonstration in the square."

"Okay, tell me about the interaction with the police."

Jack leaned forward. I could feel the intensity in his gaze, so different from his casual banter. "The first three officers we saw walked right past us. One even smiled and waved. As Officer Crane approached, Joyce whispered to me that she knew him and not in a good way. It put me on alert. He came over and immediately got belligerent. Joyce stayed calm and showed him our permit. But he got rough fast. He whipped her around and cuffed her before I knew what was happening. The rest of us started to argue with him. That's when he called for backup and the three of us got hauled in as well."

Richard took notes. "And what were the charges?"

"Resisting arrest. But what the hell were we being arrested for?"

Richard nodded his head. "Sounds like Joyce was arrested for being gay, and the rest of you got in the way."

"Exactly."

"How did *you* get out?"

Jack leaned back. "One call from my dad, I presume." He looked over at me.

I nodded.

"And the others? No arraignment yet?"

Jack shook his head. "Not yet."

"Okay." Richard leaned on his arms. "I know LGBTQ law up and down. But I don't know a damn thing about human trafficking. And while this case is really about LGBTQ rights, I need some background in trafficking, too, since that's what you were demonstrating about. I presume it is something Joyce will want to highlight when this gets big."

Jack nodded. "I can tell you what I know. But to be honest, I'm no expert either."

"I can help," I said, surprising myself almost as much as I surprised Jack.

Jack stared at me. Richard looked at me with expectation. I decided now that I'd opened my big mouth, I was committed. I'd really started it all by calling my dad. And now I was in this until Jack's friends were out of jail. If my knowledge helped make that happen, why not share it?

"I do some work for an organization in San Francisco that works on trafficking. We have lawyers who dedicate their pro-bono time to convincing the DA to prosecute the cases. We gather evidence, do detective work, interviews." I shrugged. "I've been doing research for them since undergraduate school. I can give you a brief rundown on the movement and its challenges."

Jack had a strange look on his face, a combination of shock and awe, if I had to guess. He leaned back in his chair and looked at me expectantly.

I spoke for about thirty minutes. I tried to provide a big picture of the problem. I explained that worldwide over one million people annually are deceived, sold, and transported for use as slaves, eighty percent of which are women and girls used for the sex trade, fifty percent of which are children. I talked about the problem in the US specifically, the over twenty thousand people who are trafficked into the land of the free each year. California sees just over two thousand cases a year, New York just under that number.

I talked about the movement for awareness and justice, and while I didn't know specifics about Joyce's organization, I was able to provide an overview of the basic missions and activities of organizations like hers.

When I finished, Richard thanked me and assured us we had given him what he needed to proceed. "I will have to consult with my new clients, and then I'll have some paperwork to file. But I think I can have them out tonight. I'll give you a call when we're close."

"Thanks," Jack said, standing up and shaking Richard's hand. "I want to be there when they get out."

What the hell?

"Of course," Richard said as if it were perfectly normal to potentially miss your plane home in order to watch people get out of jail.

Once we made it to the elevator, I turned on Jack. "Jack, our plane is at eight o'clock, and we *will* be on it."

He ignored that. "I knew it, Candie. I knew there was something in this world that really set you on fire."

I leaned toward him, one hand on his upper arm, and tried to put fierce intensity into my gaze, the way my nana had done to me as a child when she wanted me to behave. "Jack, did you hear me? Eight o'clock!"

The elevator stopped on the ground floor, and the doors opened. I followed Jack out to the curb. Richard had a cab waiting for us, and we both slid into it. Jack turned around on the seat to face me. "I mean, my God, Candie, you are just full of surprises."

"Seriously? So what, Jack. I know a little something about something. It's not a big deal." I folded my arms over my chest and stared straight ahead.

"A little? Candie, you have a *cause*. I knew it. I knew you were your parents' child."

I pursed my lips. "Eight o'clock."

He grinned. "Keep your panties on, Candie. We have work to do, and I'm hungry again."

****

Jack freaking Morrison was going to make me miss my plane, again. At seven o'clock, we were sitting in the lobby of the stupid jail. Richard had long since disappeared into the bowels of the building, leaving us slumped on hard wooden chairs. Jack's small black bag and the shopping bag with my cocktail dress and heels in it sat in a third uncomfortable chair beside me.

"Jack, it sounds like things are going well. Why don't we go ahead and go to the airport? I'm sure Richard will give us an update."

"Candie, you are a beautiful, smart, capable woman, but you are driving me crazy. Knock it off about the plane already."

I growled and stood up. I wanted to light into him. Instead, I turned on my heel and walked out the front door. I found a little spot just beyond the smokers and called Janice. I made a mental note to request a raise for her once she'd assured me she'd get us on the next available flight.

I stayed out there for a moment, collecting myself. Jack made me madder than any human being I'd ever met. I was, admittedly, easily frustrated. But I was also someone who prided herself on being in control, even in the most difficult situations. Jack presented a whole new challenge.

I took a deep breath. The sun setting and the humid

air slowly cooling indicated that dusk was settling over Manhattan. I'm sure most people would be reveling in the romanticism of a summer night in New York. But I just wanted to go home. Journey's song "Lights" played in my head. I wanted to be back in the City by the Bay.

I walked slowly toward the entrance to the police station, only to find that two news station vans had pulled up near the front door.

Chapter 8

When I got back to the lobby, I was greeted by Jack's empty chair. My gaze slipped around the room frantically. I had one job, to get Jack back to San Francisco. If he gave me the slip, I was going to be screwed.

Before panic could fully set in, I spotted him in a corner, huddled up with Richard and three other people, all of whom looked like they'd spent the night in jail. I walked over hesitantly, half hoping no one would notice me. No such luck.

"Candace! Come here. Meet the people you helped to free," Richard said enthusiastically.

Jack turned to look at me. An unmistakable sparkle lit up his gorgeous blue eyes. And for a split second, I wasn't pissed at him.

"Guys, this is Candie. She's a closet activist," Jack said, patting my back.

And just like that, the good feelings were gone.

"Candace Gleason. It's a pleasure to meet you," I said.

An absolutely stunningly beautiful woman stepped out of the group and approached me with her hand held out. This had to be Joyce. She was the only other woman in the room. She had long, flowing blonde hair, perfect skin, a killer figure, and eyes almost as bright blue as Jack's. If I didn't already know that she was a

74

lesbian, I would have assumed that I'd found Jack's motivation to go to jail right here.

"Thank you so much for your help," she gushed as we shook hands. "I can't tell you what it means to us. We just don't have the connections needed to find someone like Richard." She looked up at Richard as if she'd just found her savior. "And he will make all the difference."

"I'm glad everything worked out for you," I said weakly.

"Candie, did you see any press when you were out there?" Jack asked.

I would have lied. I wanted to. But it wouldn't matter, anyway. Eventually, they would be going out those doors no matter what. And while I wouldn't mind lying to Jack, especially since he made my life so freaking hard, I would feel like an ass lying to all these other people. So I nodded.

"Great," Richard said, rubbing his hands together. "Are you ready?"

Joyce, and the two men with her, all agreed they were ready to face the press. They walked toward the door in a clump, Jack close by. I grabbed our bags from the seating area and hung back. When we reached the door, I ducked to the side and managed to get completely out of camera shot. Jack, however, stayed behind Joyce.

Joyce and Richard did all the talking. Jack remained, thankfully, silent. I didn't want his face on camera, but I knew there was no way to talk him out of that. I figured his silence was the best-case scenario.

When the press circus was done and Jack had said his goodbyes, he walked back over to me. He looked like a kid who'd just walked out of a candy store with a sack stuffed full of goodies. "Okay, we can get on that plane now."

I had just finished reading a lengthy text from Janice. I looked up at Jack and, attempting to keep some of the exasperation out of my voice, I told him, "Too late. We missed that one. Janice couldn't get us another flight until six a.m."

He seemed completely unfazed by this. "Back to the Excellent Eleven then?"

"No way. Janice got us both rooms at a five-star hotel."

"I don't need to stay in a fancy hotel, Candie," he protested.

"Yeah, well, I do," I said forcefully. "And I have one job to do here: get you home. So there is no way I am letting you out of my sight until we land at SFO. Therefore, you are staying at the fancy hotel, too."

My frustration seemed to amuse him. "Okay, Candie." He held up his hands as if I were arresting him. "We'll do it your way. Take me to your stupid luxury hotel."

I wanted to slap the silly half grin off his face. Instead, I marched toward the curb to catch a cab.

****

Janice was officially my hero. Not only had she gotten me a luxurious suite with an adjoining room for Jack, she'd also arranged for a set of toiletries and a pair of cotton pajamas to be sent to my room.

I was showered, teeth brushed, and nestled into my new PJs when a knock sounded on the door to Jack's room. The PJs were full length, so, too tired to care about how they looked anyway, I went to the door as is.

Jack stood in the doorway, holding a bottle of wine and two long-stemmed glasses. He looked me up and down. "Nice jammies. I thought we should celebrate."

He looked like a fantasy I used to have. In it a gorgeous man, wearing a deep red bathrobe, stood in the doorway of a fancy hotel room holding a bottle of champagne. Jack wore the same shirt and khakis as earlier this morning and held a bottle of red wine instead of champagne, but otherwise, it was the same.

I swung the door open and stepped aside. "Sure, why not."

Jack strolled over to the kitchenette. He placed the bottle and glasses on the counter and started to work on the cork. "So how come you get the suite?"

I moved to the opposite side of the counter and sat on a wooden stool. "You wouldn't have wanted the suite. You would be more comfortable at the Excellent Eleven, remember?"

He looked up at me, piercing me with those incredible sky-colored eyes. I had one of those terrifying moments. My heart did a little flutter, like it had missed a beat or like I'd just narrowly escaped a coronary.

"As always, counselor, you are correct."

The cork popped, punctuating the tension I could feel in my stomach. Jack poured the wine. To hell with letting it breathe, I guess. He handed me a glass and held his up in the air. "To freedom and justice for all."

We clinked glasses and drank. The wine tasted good, very good. I examined the label. "Where did you get this?"

"The bar downstairs. They sell it by the bottle."

"You have good taste in wine, Jack."

Jack grabbed the other wooden stool, which sat beside me, and straddled it. "Why do you sound so surprised?"

I shrugged. "You wear twenty-dollar shoes."

He laughed. "Yes. But I grew up wearing two-hundred-dollar shoes."

"Ah, right. Sometimes I forget."

"Tell me how you got into the trafficking issue, Candie."

"Boy, you don't ever let anything go, do you?"

"Spill, counselor."

I sighed deeply, just to let him know how much of a pain in the ass I thought he was. But I told him the story, anyway. "When I was twelve, my parents took in a girl for a few months. She was thirteen at the time. Her father had sold her into slavery just after she turned eleven. She'd been brought to the US. My father was securing refugee status for her. We shared everything, my room, my clothes, everything. My parents took me out of school for that time. Sonja didn't speak much English. Instead of going to my boring classes, I got to stay home and teach her."

I stopped and took a sip of my wine, then another. This was a hard story to tell. And I hadn't intended to tell it. But I was in it now.

Jack sat still beside me, completely absorbed. He waited patiently while I took a moment, anticipation clear on his face. He leaned forward, his brow creased, his mouth slightly opened. I had to rip my eyes away from those lips.

Concentrating on the wine glass in front of me, I continued. "I loved her so much. She was like a sister to me. She told me a few things about her time as a sex slave. But not much. And I didn't really understand it until years later."

"What happened to her?"

"My father got her refugee status. Then she went to the LA area to live with some distant relatives of her mother. We went to visit a few times." I swallowed and took a deep breath. "When she was sixteen, she killed herself."

"Oh, God." His voice was soft. "Candie, I'm sorry." Jack placed his hand over mine.

I didn't move my left hand. I used my right to finish my glass of wine. Jack used his other hand to pour me more. We sat there for a while, drinking wine and holding hands.

"So that's why," he finally said.

"Yeah, that's why." I deflated my lungs and moved my hand out from under Jack's. Trying to regain my composure, I sat straighter. "What about you, Jack?"

"What about me?"

Damn him. One minute he acted sweet and cooperative, the next he was back to being an evasive ass. "Okay, for starters, where were you for those missing five years?"

Jack took his time finishing his own glass of wine, then poured himself more. "Nope. Not gonna tell that one yet. How about the story of why I chose to work on housing issues?"

I sighed. "Okay, fine. Let's hear it."

He chuckled. "You sound disappointed."

"Because, Jack, I think that's obvious."

"Really?"

"Yeah."

"Okay, counselor. Then what's the story?"

"Your family was in the business. You saw the dark side of it and turned your back on it. You went away for a little 'you time,' and when you came back, you decided to dedicate yourself to undoing the misery your family caused."

He shook his head. "Pretty close. But I think Delores deserves mention."

"Delores?"

"Yes, the woman who lived on my porch when I was in college. I lived in a condo in a building my family's business had built. I usually ignored her. She was kind of a novelty, you know, the crazy lady who lived on my porch. Sometimes I gave her my leftover food. My friends all knew about her. We'd laugh about Delores."

Jack started to play with the stem of his wine glass, rolling it in his fingers. And for the first time since the moment I'd met him, his posture showed discomfort. "One night, I came home in a bad mood. I'd been out late the night before, and I went to my class hung over. I'd completely blown an important test. The girl I'd been sleeping with for the last couple of weeks was getting overly attached, and I knew I would have to break it off with her soon. So when I saw Delores sitting there on my porch next to my front door, I unleashed my anger on her. I don't even remember what I said exactly, but I screamed at her and told her to get the fuck off my porch. And she left."

Jack ran a hand through his hair. "A few days went by, and I didn't see her again. I don't know why, but it started to bug me. Every time I walked in or out of my apartment, it would eat away at me. After a week with no sign of her, I went down to the police station and asked about her. Turns out the night I kicked her off my porch, she went to sleep under a bridge. Some other homeless people found her dead the next morning. No one knew exactly what had killed her. No one cared. I cared." He thumped his chest with two fingers. "I cared a lot. I started to research Delores."

Jack paused, taking a few deep breaths. This time I placed my hand on his. "What did you find out?"

"She had lived in the tenement building that Morrison tore down to build the condos. She moved in with her husband when she was seventeen years old. She raised her kids there, three of them. Two of her kids died in infancy. Her husband died, too. Her surviving son ended up in jail. She was all alone when I met her. Her apartment had been right there where my porch was."

"When they evicted her, she didn't get anything?"

"She did. She got a few thousand dollars. But it wasn't anywhere near enough to get anything in the area. She would have had to move at least thirty minutes away. But you see, her husband and her two children were buried at the cemetery just up the road. She couldn't be that far away from them. So she stayed in a hotel nearby until the money ran out. Then she was left with just her social security. It was enough to feed her but not enough to afford housing in that neighborhood, not after the gentrification."

"And her death? Did you ever find out about that?"

"No." He shook his head and finally looked at me again. "They cremated her and buried her in some unmarked grave in a city plot. So, no autopsy. I was, however, able to get her moved."

"Moved?"

"I had her buried in the cemetery with her family. As soon as I made sure the headstone was installed, I left town."

I, of course, wanted to ask him where he went. But now was not the time. Instead, I blinked back the tears his story had conjured and poured more wine for us both.

Chapter 9

When I opened my eyes, I was not sure if I was really awake. After all, I had been dreaming about Jack Morrison, and here he was, lying right beside me.

Holy shit!

I sat up so fast I jostled the bed, the bed I lay on with Jack Morrison. He started to move. I jumped off the bed. Jack stirred some more and opened his eyes.

I ran my hands over myself, unable to break my gaze from Jack. My sleep clothes seemed to be completely intact.

"Hey," he said, in a sexy, groggy tone. When I realized that he was lying on top of the covers, completely clothed, I started to breathe again. Jack sat up on his elbows. "Why do you look like that?"

"Like what?"

"Panicked."

I tried to pull myself together. "I'm fine. I was just surprised you were still here when I woke up is all."

"We drank two bottles of wine last night. But I would think you would remember, Candie."

"Two?"

"Yeah, we went and got another bottle. Then we watched *Office Space*. I think I fell asleep before it ended." He sat up and swung his legs over the side of the bed. "You don't remember?"

I did. Now. It was coming back. I remembered

walking down to the bar with Jack in my pajamas to get the second bottle of wine. I remembered laughing about it. Which is so unlike me. I remembered drinking more wine and watching the movie. It was all there. The panic must have given me temporary amnesia.

"Yeah, I remember." I turned away from him and grabbed my clothes from yesterday. "I'm, uh, I'm going to take a shower now. See you in a bit." And then I escaped behind the bathroom door.

Once safely behind closed doors, I sank onto the closed toilet seat. My God, what had I gotten myself in to? Last night I'd befriended Jack Morrison. Jack Morrison my assignment. Jack Morrison my boss's boss's son. Jack Morrison my archnemesis. Crap.

****

When I met back up with Jack an hour later, he was the same old grinning, obnoxious man I'd known before I'd stupidly gotten drunk with him. "I think we missed our plane again."

"Yes, we did. But I've already made us new arrangements," I said tersely.

"Do we have time for breakfast?"

"Yes, but we're eating at the airport. This is our fourth flight, and we *are not* missing it."

"Yes, ma'am. Lead the way."

I turned and walked stiffly to the elevator. I was going to be nothing but professional with Jack Morrison from here on out. Everything I did, from the tone of my voice to my body language, would be a message to Jack to stay professional. This relationship was going to be purely business.

Jack didn't seem to get the hint, however. No matter how cold I acted toward him all through the airport and all through the six-hour flight, he continued to be kind, congenial, and amused. It was really irritating.

I didn't arrive at the office until late afternoon on Monday. But I walked in with my head held high, my mission accomplished.

"I see you managed to make it back," Tom Garrity said as he walked into my office ten minutes after I'd returned.

"I did. Yes."

"What took so long? John and I expected you back on Sunday."

Jesus, did this guy not realize what a complete and utter miracle it was that I'd managed to get Jack back at all?

"We ran into a few hiccups with the flights. But we made it back without any further run-ins with the police."

Garrity grunted at me before walking out of my office without another word. No "thank you." No "job well done." No "sorry I ruined your entire weekend." I sank my head in my hands. Jack Morrison was going to be the death of me.

I was delighted when, just after five, I received an email from Tom asking me to help Joseph with his project. Thankful for the distraction, I called Joseph right away to set up a meeting to go over the project and determine what assistance I could provide. We set the meeting for nine the next morning. I left the office just after seven feeling like, for the first time since Kent had laid that folder on my desk last week, I had something to look forward to.

****

Kay Harris

The good news was Joseph's project would be an excuse to spend less time with Jack Morrison. The bad news was Joseph's project directly involved Jack Morrison. Joseph was trying to fight the historic designation on the Baldy building that Jack had filed. And that kind of Karma was par for the course for me lately.

But I dove into the project headfirst. My job consisted mainly of research, something I excelled at. So I read everything I could get my hands on about historic laws. I made calls to city officials, architects, and historians. And for three full days I pretended Jack Morrison didn't exist.

Things were going well in my personal life, too. I went to dinner at my parents' house on Wednesday, and there was no man sitting there waiting to be fixed up with me. It was just me and my folks. In fact, my mother didn't even discuss the search for my soul mate. My dad and I talked about New York. My father exuded so much pride, I nearly blushed. It felt good.

On Thursday, Hayden asked me out again. He wanted to take his rain check on Saturday night, and I accepted. So, on Friday morning when Joseph sat me down and asked me to do something terrible, I felt betrayed by fate.

"We need you to meet with Jack Morrison," Joseph said the minute I sat across from him in his office.

"Okay. About Baldy, I take it?"

"Yes."

"Okay, well, I can certainly ask him what his plans are, but I have to be honest, I doubt he's going to be forthcoming. The thing about Jack is—"

"I don't want *you* to be forthcoming."

"Excuse me?"

"Look, you're supposed to be meeting with him regularly anyway, right?"

I nodded.

"Kent seemed to think once a week was a good expectation. Is that what you're doing?"

"Well, I just got the assignment last week, Joseph. But, yes, that's a reasonable expectation."

Except I hadn't met with Jack this week. In fact, I had ignored the three emails he'd sent me.

"Okay, so use those routine meetings to get as much information as you can without Jack realizing it. In fact, if you can meet in his office, that might be the most helpful. Kent says it's open concept. I'll bet you can overhear all kinds of stuff in there."

I became distinctly uncomfortable. Not only was it not Joseph's job to tell me how to operate as it pertained to Jack, but what he was asking me to do crossed the line from babysitter to spy. I decided to force him to clarify exactly his instructions. "So, you're asking me to obtain information on Jack's operations using covert and dishonest methods?"

"Yep," he said casually. "I thought that was sort of a given." He looked at me expectantly.

I wholeheartedly disagreed. I'd never been tasked with that by my boss. It was my job to keep Jack out of trouble, not to sabotage his work. "Has this been run by Garrity?"

"Candace, this comes all the way from the top." He pointed to the ceiling. "I'm not asking you to change any of the other directives you've been given about Jack. Just find out what he's up to on Baldy. That's all we're asking."

I really didn't know what to say. The whole thing rubbed me the wrong way. What could I do about it? I was, without a doubt, the low woman on this totem pole. I needed to do what I was told to keep my position at the company. So, I agreed and headed back to my office to finally answer Jack's email. I kept it very professional.

Dear Jack,

I would like to request a meeting with you this afternoon. We can meet at your office if that is most convenient for you. Please respond with your time preference.

Sincerely,

Candace Gleason

Jack responded ten minutes later.

I can't meet today. How about tomorrow?

I wrote back.

Dear Jack,

I would be happy to meet with you tomorrow. What time shall I come to your office?

Sincerely,

Candace Gleason

He wrote back within five minutes.

Meet me at my apartment at 9 a.m.

I didn't like the idea of meeting at Jack's apartment. I needed to keep things with him completely on the up and up. But nailing Jack down had proven to be hard in the past, and I knew better than to turn down any offer he gave me. So I responded.

Dear Jack,

I will meet you outside your apartment at 9 a.m. tomorrow (Saturday).

Sincerely,

Candace Gleason

His answer was simple.

Fine.

I wondered if I was screwing this up by being distant. Jack clearly wanted to be friends. Maybe I would get further with him that way. Charming and personable, Jack was the kind of man who sucked a person in and made her feel comfortable and at home. He was the kind of man that could get you drunk and make you go to a bar in pajamas. That was dangerous— very, very dangerous—especially for someone like me.

An introvert who kept most people at arm's length, I had exactly two friends in the whole world. I prided myself on keeping everything above board and purely professional with everyone in my career life.

But Jack was just the opposite. He was surrounded by people who were close to him. He treated his staff like they were his friends, and he cozied up to practically every damn person he met on the street, as evidenced by his insta-friends in New York. With Jack, taking a casual approach would get me much more information than being standoffish.

But it didn't really matter which method was going to be the most effective in getting Jack to cooperate, or in getting information out of him, because the bottom line was I couldn't afford to get close to Jack. When I let my guard down around him, all hell broke loose. I'd befriended Jack in New York and managed to involve myself in getting some hippies out of jail, come back a day late, and gotten drunk and wound up in the same bed with my dangerously hot babysittee.

No, I could not be friends with Jack Morrison, no matter what.

Chapter 10

I stood outside Jack's door. Despite the fact that it was Saturday morning, I wore a navy-blue pant suit and brown pumps, my hair pulled back in a bun. I carried my briefcase. I was sending a message to Jack. I was a complete professional.

Jack came down to the porch after I buzzed him and refused to come up. He looked me up and down casually, then smirked. But he didn't comment on my attire or how it clashed with his jeans, T-shirt, and sandals.

He carried a light jacket in his arms, like all good Bay Area residents, and a water bottle. "You want that briefcase?" he asked me. "Or do you want to ditch it inside?"

"I thought we would go to a restaurant to meet."

"We'll eat eventually. But we're gonna walk around a bit first. Doubt you wanna carry that thing all over the city."

"Seriously?"

He turned away from me and gazed out at the cityscape. "Take it or leave it."

"Fine." I dug my cell phone out of the briefcase and put it in the pocket of my blazer before handing the bag to Jack.

He grinned, took it from me, and ran back upstairs. When he returned, the jacket he'd been holding hung on his lean and sturdy frame, and he looked for all the world like a man who'd just won an epic battle.

"Come on," Jack said, moving past me and down the sidewalk.

I followed him, the thick click-click of my pumps echoing back to my ears as I worked to keep up with his long strides. A part of me realized we were going deeper into the Tenderloin. And my reaction was to stay as close to Jack as I could. My breathing grew louder in my ears and the sound of my shoes on the concrete seemed to grow impossibly faster.

When we rounded a corner and saw a mass of young men with baggy pants and bandanas on their heads, I started to panic a little. I reached out and grabbed hold of Jack's arm.

That's the moment everything changed. One minute, I'd practically been chasing him down the sidewalk in cold silence. But as soon as I touched him, Jack slowed down. He pulled up next to me so that we were walking side by side, and he took my hand in his.

I knew I shouldn't be allowing this. But in that moment my brain wasn't capable of figuring out what, exactly, I should be doing instead. And I was still panicking over the group of kids who were headed straight for us.

It wasn't their appearance that made me apprehensive. Hell, they looked a lot better than the people my mom had over for dinner. It was their age and their noisiness. They were shouting obscenities to one another as they walked down the street. And I'd seen enough TV crime dramas to know that this was how the episode always started. Next, the rowdy youths would come up and start harassing us.

Jack was not in the least bit worried. In fact, he broke our silence and started talking. "This is a very old neighborhood. It dates back to the Gold Rush. Most of it was destroyed in 1906. But they rebuilt right away."

As he talked, I watched the kids. There were three of them, one staring hard at me. He raked his gaze up and down, and a lascivious grin painted his face. They paid absolutely no attention to Jack. They focused completely on me.

Jack stopped on the sidewalk. Taking my shoulders in his hands, he turned me to face him. "Are you all right?"

I nodded weakly, my eyes darting to the side to see the kids. We shouldn't have stopped. Wouldn't that only invite them to stop, too?

Jack examined me for a minute. "Are you sure you are the daughter of Robert and Lily?"

I rolled my eyes at him.

"Haven't you ever been down here before?"

"Sure. When I was kid. My parents had friends who lived down here."

"And were you this nervous then?"

Jesus, I couldn't believe he was talking about this now. Those kids were actually in hearing range.

"No," I said as defiantly as I could manage.

The kids were right next to us now. The one who'd been grinning at me slowed his pace, his eyes still pawing at me. "Hey," he called.

Jack looked up at him and gave a half wave. "Hey." Then he turned back to me. The kids kept right on walking. "What happened to you between childhood and adulthood, Candie?"

I wrenched my shoulders out of his grip and looked

back at the kids again. "Why were they so focused on me?" I asked him. "They barely seemed to notice you."

"Well, for starters, you're wearing a suit in the Tenderloin on a Saturday morning. They probably think you're on your way to evict someone. You're clearly nervous as hell. Which is only inviting someone to fuck with you, really. And you're hot."

I didn't know how to respond to that, so I turned on my heel, facing the sidewalk stretching ahead of us. "Come on, show me what you were going to show me already."

Jack dragged me all through the Tenderloin, telling me about the neighborhood's history and pointing out prominent historic buildings. We stopped at the Cadillac Hotel and sat down for a little while, which my feet were extraordinarily grateful for. Jack didn't look the least bit fazed by the walking or the wind that had been constantly whipping us since we'd left his apartment. And it was apparent that he'd stopped for me.

While we sat there, Jack told me all about the Cadillac. Built as a high-end hotel just after the big quake, now a nonprofit organization ran it. They provided housing to those in need and held concerts and community events in its historic ballroom.

To Jack, the Cadillac stood as a shining example of what could be done in this city. His face lit up when he talked about it. His hands flailed around. His whole body seemed to be alive with electricity. And I couldn't look away.

After our brief stop, I tried to end this little tour by telling Jack I was hungry. So he took me to the heart of the Tenderloin for Indian food. It was amazing. It might have been the best Indian food I'd ever had, though I would never tell my mother that.

I relaxed after that. Jack and I walked around some more, and it was me who pulled him into an art gallery.

"What's your thing, Candie?" he asked, walking up behind me to gaze at the photograph I was stuck in front of.

"I like lots of different kinds of art," I told him. "Photos, landscapes, classic pieces. But I guess, based on the amount of time I spend at MOMA, I like the abstract stuff best." I shrugged. "I don't know. I like it all."

"Why?" He stood much closer to me than I'd realized. His breath hit my neck as he leaned down toward my ear.

I shivered a little, hoping that Jack didn't notice. "I like the idea of making things with your hands. And I love the idea that it all comes from somewhere inside the artist. It's like they put their soul on canvas, or paper, or clay."

"What kind of art do you do?"

I turned around, realizing too late how very close we'd be when I did. "I don't. I mean, I'm not an artist. I just appreciate art. My friend Meg is, though. She's very talented."

"I bet you are, too," he whispered.

The way he'd said that, his face so near my own, his day-old stubble and full lips tempting me, it was too much. So I brushed past him and walked briskly out onto the street.

Chapter 11

As we headed back to his apartment. Jack and I ran into about a dozen people he knew. A few looked like him, young, casually dressed, and idealistic. A few were homeless. Jack spoke to them just like he did with everyone else and dropped a few dollars subtly into their hands. A few of the people he talked with looked downright terrifying. Jack chatted with each person for a few minutes and introduced me. They were all very nice. But they looked at me as if I was a serious oddity, and they were trying to figure out what to make of me.

By the time we got back to his place, I realized I hadn't gotten an iota of useful information out of him. Sunset painted the city. Jack and I had spent the whole day walking through the fifty blocks of the Tenderloin, talking, eating, looking at art and buildings. I had to admit I'd enjoyed myself. But I had not accomplished my mission. So when Jack suggested that I come up for a drink, I took him up on it.

During the elevator ride, I remembered I was supposed to be across town meeting Hayden for our date. When we stepped out into the hallway, I paused. "Um...hey, I need to make a quick phone call."

"Sure." Jack opened the door to his apartment and extended his arm. "You can use the den."

I walked past him. "There's a den?"

He chuckled. "Yep. Around the corner."

I headed to the end of the living room and was surprised to find a short, narrow hallway hiding beside the bedroom. I walked down it and through the open sliding wooden door into a cozy den.

"It's a little 1970s in there," Jack called as I looked around the room. "But I kinda like it that way, so I haven't updated it."

All four paneled walls held mounted light fixtures and built-in recessed shelving. A large window sat above a throwback metal desk. The desk, an odd shade of light green, the color of an old hospital, stood neat and uncluttered. It held only a printer, a few wires awaiting a laptop computer, and a mug filled with pens. Shelves lined with books and folders were well stacked and organized.

I sat down in the winged desk chair and pulled out my cell phone. I felt like a heel as I dialed Hayden.

"Candace? I'm on my way to the restaurant now. You're not waiting there for me already, are you?" Hayden asked as soon as he answered.

"No, Hayden. Actually, I'm calling to tell you I can't make it."

I counted my breaths as the pause drew out. Finally, Hayden spoke. "Again?"

"I'm so sorry, Hayden. Something came up."

"Is it my brother again? Is he in lock-up somewhere?"

I wanted to balance honesty with my deep desire not to get into details. "No jail this time," I said, letting my voice take on the tone of frustration I usually used when talking about Jack.

"Huh. That's a pleasant surprise, I guess. Well, okay. Let's, um, try again soon then. Maybe we can actually find some time when my big brother doesn't ruin everything."

I laughed lightly. "Deal."

"Take care, Candace. And let me know if I can help. Though, when it comes to Jack, I'm usually not helpful. We just end up fighting, and then things get worse." Hayden chuckled. "Call me."

"Will do. Goodbye, Hayden."

After I hung up, I stayed in Jack's den for a minute and took several deep breaths. I looked at the pictures hanging on the walls. Two were oil paintings, old school landscapes of some kind. The rest were photos of people.

I got up and walked over to the closest picture. About two dozen people stood in four rows in front of the Homes Without Inc. offices. I recognized a few of them and realized it was a staff picture.

I moved on to the next photo. Two women, both in wedding dresses, stood in the center of the photo with people of both genders on either side of them. I saw Jack standing beside a woman I recognized from his office. He wore a tux, and he had a massive smile on his face.

The last picture in the room, right beside the door, was of Jack's family. Jack was probably about ten years old in the picture. They were clearly on vacation somewhere. Having not traveled extensively and barely having passed geography, I wasn't sure where. But wherever it was, the ocean framed the background of a happy family. Jack's parents stood with their arms around each other. Hayden and Chelsea were both sitting in the foreground on the beach, their attention focused on a pile of muddy sand between them that they were shaping with their hands. Jack kneeled beside Chelsea. His bright blue eyes twinkled in the sun. His bleached hair swept across his forehead. He stuck his tongue out at the picture-taker. He looked happy.

I ripped my eyes away from the photo and walked back to the living room. Jack was in the kitchen as I came in. I nestled into the comfy couch and flipped off my shoes. I knew it was unprofessional, but after all that walking, my feet were killing me. I leaned back in my seat and put my legs out in front of me, my heels resting on the carpet, my toes up in the air.

"Wine?" Jack asked from the kitchen.

"A nice white would be good right now," I suggested. I wondered idly if I was taxing Jack. Would he have a variety of wines in his house?

I heard the refrigerator open and close, followed by the pop of a cork. Then Jack walked into the living room, placed a bottle of white wine and two long-stemmed glasses on the coffee table and took a seat right next to me on the couch.

"Your feet hurt?" he asked, eyeing my bare toes.

"A little."

"That's what you get for walking around the city in impractical shoes."

"I didn't know I would be walking around the city," I pointed out.

"Give 'em here."

I gaped at him. "What?"

He gestured with his hand. "Your feet. Put them up here." He patted his thigh.

"Why?"

"Because I'm going to rub them," he said as if this were the most obvious thing in the world.

I'd woken up in bed next to Jack, I'd let him hold my hand, and now this. I had been crossing way too many lines, and I wasn't ready to cross another one. "Maybe I should go," I said, shifting in my seat.

Jack cocked one eyebrow at me. "You want information?"

I sighed. "Yes. I *need* something before I go back to work on Monday," I told him honestly

He patted his thigh again. "Well, then."

Jack's games should have me so pissed off I couldn't see straight. I should be running away from this man as far as I could. After all, he'd done nothing but toy with me since I'd met him. But for some reason, I wasn't angry. I was mostly intrigued.

I swung myself around on the couch and plopped my feet onto his leg. Jack immediately enclosed my left foot in both of his hands. "Good girl."

I scooted further down on the couch and laid my head back on the arm. I involuntarily let out a little groan as his fingers kneaded my muscles and caressed my skin.

"Does that feel better?"

"Yes. But I should feel bad right now. My feet are kind of…nasty."

"Hmm. They're just fine."

My eyes closed, and my entire body completely relaxed for the first time in years. "Please don't tell me you have some sort of foot fetish," I teased.

He chuckled. "No. But I do have a thing for legs. And Candie, you have amazing legs."

I didn't open my eyes. I couldn't. I was too blissed out at that moment. So, instead of finding out what I needed to know by simply looking at Jack, I asked him instead, "Are you staring at them right now?"

I could feel that my pants had ridden up on my calves, and I knew I was exposing a little bit of skin. Then I felt the material on my left leg rise even higher.

"Yep. It's even better when you wear skirts. But right now, I'm getting a real eyeful, so I won't complain."

I should have been completely upset with this exchange. But I wasn't. "Lucky for you, I shaved."

One of Jack's hands moved slowly up my ankle. His fingers were slightly calloused and the friction on my skin was a foreign sensation. What little experience I had was with men with soft hands, men who worked with computers all day. Jack's hands had clearly seen some real work. And I found myself reveling in the sensation as his palm moved slowly up to my calf.

The entire thing took forever, every movement from Jack in slow motion. The experience was reminiscent of the soft porn part of a movie. No way in hell I intended to stop it.

"You have the softest skin," he said in a low voice.

"You are going to be the death of me, Jack Morrison," I groaned.

His hand made its way to my knee before the slacks were too tight for him to continue. I stayed still, not wanting to move, not wanting the things I was feeling to go away. Jack's legs shifted under me and then the heat of him beat down on me from above. I opened my eyes and Jack's face hovered over mine.

One clump of hair flopped over his left eye. I wanted to get a better look at those stark blue eyes, so I reached up and pushed it out of the way. Then I let my fingers run down his temple, over his cheekbone, and down to the coarse hair on his chin.

"I'm supposed to be drilling you for information," I said softly. "I'm not doing a very good job."

"Hmm. Tell you what. I'll give you access to my Google calendar if you stop worrying about your job for a minute."

"Okay," I breathed.

Jack leaned down, just as slowly as his hand had moved up my leg. And when his lips met mine, I immediately opened up for him. It was instinct, pure and simple. Jack took advantage, sweeping his tongue along mine.

I arched forward to get more of him. This seemed to spur an immediate reaction. He pulled us both farther down on the couch so I was fully beneath him. His arm supported his weight on the cushion beside my head, and I ran my hand over it. He had these wonderfully developed biceps that made my stomach flutter.

I was on fire just then. My attraction for Jack had built up and now burned in a hot, heavy flame. And I wanted more. I wanted so much more. I wanted to strip this man naked and touch every part of him.

The thought shocked me. So I stopped.

I closed my lips and gave Jack a gentle push. He immediately climbed off me and sat back on the couch. He ran a hand through his hair and pushed a heavy sigh through his lips. "Is your computer in there?" he asked, gesturing to my briefcase.

What the hell was this about? "Yes."

"Bring it to me."

I was on autopilot at that moment. My brain had completely stalled out. I just did what I was told. I stood up, walked over to where my briefcase sat on the counter, and retrieved my computer. I walked back over to the couch, and standing in front of him, I handed it over. He opened it up and asked me to type in my password.

"It's sandradayo," I said stoically.

He looked at me for a long moment. But if he recognized the reference to the former Supreme Court Justice I idolized, he didn't say it. Instead, he turned back to the screen. I watched as he did something on my laptop, then folded it closed and handed it back to me.

"There, I've shared my calendar with you."

"Um…thank you." I shoved the computer back in my bag and started to make my way toward the door.

As I passed Jack, he reached out and grabbed my hand. "I'm not sorry," he said before releasing me.

I got the hell out of there and headed home.

****

By noon Sunday, I was still in my pajamas. I'd spent the morning drinking coffee, searching through my kitchen for nonexistent food, and trying to stay focused on the project I'd been working on. I couldn't stomach the research I'd been tasked with at Morrison lately. Instead of getting further along on that over the weekend, like I should have been, I'd been looking into a human-trafficking resolution recently made by the UN.

After a few hours on the computer, I finally decided to shower and get dressed so I could feel human again. I was just closing the laptop when my eye caught the calendar app. I snuggled the computer back on my lap and opened it up.

Jack had shared his private calendar with me. It

was not his public Homes Without Inc. calendar as I had assumed it would be. Everything was noted on there. All of his meetings were marked and included notes about what they would be on. All of his media appearances and planned protests identified. Even a dentist appointment was marked. I scrolled through it week after week in awe. Jack had given me the kind of information that could be used to completely torpedo him and his organization. He had trusted me with it. All for one kiss.

I hit the Today button and saw that at ten o'clock Jack had a reoccurring event. My jaw dropped. "Brunch with fam," it said. This man spent his weekdays trying to sabotage his family's company and then had a cozy brunch with them every Sunday?

Then I realized I was jumping to conclusions. "Fam" didn't necessarily mean the Morrisons. After all, I had about a dozen aunts and uncles who weren't technically family at all. To my parents, the activist community was family. Perhaps Jack's idea of brunch with family consisted of hanging out with a group of friends or maybe even his employees. He seemed like the "we're all a family here" kind of boss.

I'd just set the laptop on the table and headed toward the bathroom when my phone rang. I didn't bother looking at who was calling as I answered. I assumed it was one of my parents. They called me every Sunday.

"Hello."

"Hi, Candie."

"Jack…um…hi."

"Beautiful morning, isn't it? Well, afternoon now, I guess."

I didn't know why he called me, but it gave me the chance to satisfy my curiosity about his standing brunch date. "Where are you?"

"Driving over the Bay Bridge."

"Um...why?"

"I just had brunch at the Morrison mansion, and I always find that a little taxing. So I was planning to take a walk in the redwoods."

I was still processing the fact that he did, indeed, have brunch with his family every Sunday. Then I realized that he was headed to the East Bay at that very moment. A lovely regional park sat at the edge of Oakland filled with younger redwood trees, and the tourists didn't know about it. I walked there myself on occasion.

"Despite the appearance you try to keep up of a prissy, hoity-toity lawyer-type, I bet you secretly dig the outdoors."

I wanted to be offended. But it was actually true. I'd spent my childhood camping and hiking, and I still loved to do those things. But I didn't tell anyone.

"Meet me there," Jack suggested.

"Right now?"

"Yeah."

I should have said no. Instead, I said, "Give me half an hour."

Chapter 12

Jack looked hotter than hell leaned up against the gate of a pickup truck in his jeans and T-shirt, his unruly hair blowing in the slight breeze, his eyes glowing in the sun.

"Is that what you wear to brunch with your mother?" I asked as I got out of my car and made my way over to him.

"Yep. She doesn't care." He shrugged. "After five years of me being gone, she'll take me however she can get me."

I stopped in front of him. I wore hiking boots instead of heels, so he was much higher up than usual now. "I bet she was worried."

He nodded.

"Don't you feel bad that you put her through that?"

"Of course I do. I feel bad for putting Chelsea and my dad, and maybe even Hayden, through it, too. But I had to do it to become the person I am today. I hope they love me enough to understand that someday."

"Where were you?" I asked again.

"I'll tell you later. Let's walk."

He held his hand out to me. When I didn't immediately take it, he wiggled his fingers. I relented and put my hand in his as I followed him onto the trail.

"Why are your hands calloused?" I asked.

"I use them a lot," he explained. "I do projects at

the apartment complex, help out some buddies working to renovate other buildings, stuff like that."

"Figures."

"Some women find a man that works with his hands to be sexy," he said, rubbing his thumb along the inside of my wrist.

"And some women find a man in a suit sexy," I retorted.

"Hmm. I bet I can guess which one you are, Candie."

"Why do you call me Candie?"

"I like it. It suits you. And I like that I'm the only one who calls you that."

"You're not."

He stopped on the path and cocked his head at me. "I'm not?"

"No. My dad calls me that. When you first did it, I thought maybe you knew him."

"Hmm. Maybe I should stop then."

For reasons I would probably never comprehend, I didn't want him to. "Why?"

Suddenly, Jack pulled me into his arms and moved us both off the trail until my back was up against a giant tree. My head spun as I looked up at him, my breath shallow, my eyes wide.

"I don't want you to think about your dad when you're with me," he said, lowering his head.

I put my hands on either side of his face. He was freshly shaven today, and his skin was deliciously smooth. "I don't," I told him.

Then, he was kissing me again. I angled my head to deepen the kiss and moved my hands over his broad shoulders, down his hard sides and to the bottom of his shirt. He rested his hands on my waist, then moved them lower to cup my ass. I plunged my tongue into his mouth and my hands up into his shirt. His stomach and chest were just as toned as his arms, and when I reached the tuft of hair between his nipples, I gave it a little tug.

Jack moaned and moved his head back to look at me. "Take me back to your place," he pleaded. I was having an internal war with myself, and Jack could see it in my eyes. "I'll tell you about the five years I was gone. All of it. I'll tell you what no one else in the States knows."

"Why is everything a negotiation between us?" I asked him.

"You tell me?"

I couldn't answer that question. I could barely breathe at that moment. My brain was working enough to know that taking Jack back to my house was a terrible idea. But at that moment, I couldn't bring myself to care. "Okay, we can go to my apartment," I said softly.

****

I didn't give much thought to my horrible decision as we wandered back to the parking lot hand in hand. Jack and I had talked lightly about the redwoods. Then I got into my car, and as Jack followed me back to my apartment, panic started to set in.

A dangerous path stretched in front of me. I wanted Jack Morrison in a way I couldn't ever remember wanting a man before. But this attraction between us could mean losing the career I'd been working toward all my life. It was stupid. So stupid.

By the time we reached my place, I'd decided I would hear Jack's story. We'd drink some lemonade and talk for a bit. Then I'd kick him out. Jack had proven last night that he easily complied with my wishes. I knew if I told him to go, he would.

Feeling more confident about the plan than I had any right to, I took Jack up to my apartment. He looked around with appreciation as I poured two glasses of lemonade and set out a plate of cookies on the coffee table. After examining the crown molding on my ceiling, he sat beside me on the couch.

Damn. I'd already made mistake number one. I should have sat in the chair so this couldn't happen. We were in the exact same position we'd been in the night before when we'd started making out.

Jack reached over and casually brushed a lock of hair off my cheek, tucking it behind my ear. "I already told you about Delores."

I nodded.

"After that happened, I had a crisis of conscience. I tried to talk to my dad about it, but he just gave me these corporate lines. My mom doesn't know anything about the business, and she likes it that way. I went to her next, but she was no help either. It was my uncle James who told me I should take a vacation and get it all off my mind. Of course, he meant I should take off to Cabo or something for a few weeks, party like a rich kid, and forget the less fortunate. Instead, I went to Rio de Janeiro."

"You went to Brazil?"

"Yeah. My college roommate, Meno, lives there."

"Meno?"

He chuckled. "Yeah. His parents were both history professors. They named him Menelaus, but he goes by Meno for short. Anyway, Meno's a free spirit. He always did what he wanted. In the middle of our second year of college, his parents died suddenly, and he kind of went off the deep end. He took the life insurance money and went to Rio to open a North American restaurant."

"North American? What does he do, serve burgers?"

"Pretty much, but he charges a fortune for them. And people pay." He laughed. "The guy is something else."

"So you went to stay with this guy?"

"Yeah. For the first year and a half, I helped Meno open his restaurant. Once he was set up and doing well, I would take off for months at time. I would go to other areas in Brazil. I worked with a few different groups on volunteer projects. When I ran out of money, I'd go back to Rio and work at the restaurant until I had enough cash to do it again. I lived like that for five years. I was having a crisis of conscience. I needed to find my own way, and using my trust fund was completely out of the question. It hurt me to even think about it." He shrugged. "So, thanks to Meno, I could do what I needed to do to figure out my shit."

"He sounds like a good guy."

"He is. And if it wasn't for him, I'm not sure how it all would have turned out."

"Did your parents know where you were?"

"I called them right away. And I called every couple of months to let them know I was all right. But I never promised to come home. In fact, for the first few years, I intended to never go home at all."

"What changed?"

"I started to feel like a coward. I was running.

That's all I was doing. If I really wanted to change the situation for people like Delores, I had to face it head on. So I spent time making plans, making contacts, all from Rio. Then, when I felt I was ready to face the city again and open Homes Without Inc., I flew back. I set up the office and started recruiting employees and volunteers the next day. My trust fund got its first attention in five years."

"And your family was…what? Happy you were back? Pissed about what you'd decided to do upon your return?"

"Both." Jack played with my hair, looping it around his fingers. "Candie, do you have any idea how beautiful you are? I'm not giving you a line. I swear. It's just…I'm kind of in awe that I'm sitting here with you right now. You are so stunning."

I had no idea how to react to that. So I didn't. I just stared at him.

"Have you had a lot of boyfriends?"

I shook my head.

"No? I guess I shouldn't be surprised. You've been focused on your career."

"A career I'm jeopardizing right now," I said to remind both him and myself of the gravity of the situation.

Jack leaned in. "I swear I don't want that," he said softly. "I want you to have everything you desire."

I shivered at the seduction dripping from his voice. "Even if what I want goes against your own goals?"

"It's a tough thing for sure. And don't think I'm not struggling with it. But maybe…yes. I gave you my calendar. That was a dumb move."

"So…" I moved my hand to his thigh and

squeezed. It was thick and hard, and I wanted to see what his legs looked like without jeans "You make a dumb move, then I make a dumb move, and...what? We try to help each other not let those dumb moves hurt us."

"Precisely. And we have to trust each other."

"Should I lie to my boss?" I asked, already knowing that there was no way I was going to kick Jack out of my apartment.

"We'll figure something out," he whispered, just before his lips crashed against mine.

I tugged on Jack, pulling him closer to me as we kissed. I knew this time, it wouldn't end until we were both completely satisfied.

A few minutes after the kissing started, I managed to pull myself away from him and stand. I held out my hand. "Come to my bedroom, Jack."

He smiled and followed me down the short hallway to my room. I loved my room, and I watched as Jack took it in. An old quilt that a woman at a peace rally had given to me when I was five lay across my bed. A vintage dresser and matching end table stood across the room from each other. Gauzy material I'd gotten at a street fair covered the ample window. It perfectly complemented the quilt.

"You are full of surprises," Jack said, pulling me back into his arms.

While we kissed, I pulled Jack's clothes off him and he gently divested me of mine until we were both naked. Then we tumbled onto the bed. At some point, we ended up lying side by side. And Jack stopped kissing me for a moment.

He was staring at me, just staring, as his fingers

played in my most sensitive of places. I was trying to breathe, my gaze locked on Jack's blue eyes. Then he pushed a finger inside me.

I arched my back. "God, Jack," I cried.

"You are amazing," he whispered.

"You're killing me," I told him, gripping his ass.

"Tell me what you want, Candie."

"I want more, Jack," I groaned. "More."

Chapter 13

Present day—Rio
Jack

"Wait, back up. You fell for a lawyer? A lawyer with your dad's company? What the hell, Jack?"

I should have expected this reaction. When I'd arrived here six days ago, I wouldn't talk about it. I told my friend I needed time. Now, we're sitting in his living room after a long day at the restaurant, and I'm spilling the whole story on him.

He's surprised enough that I ran all the way to Rio over a woman. When I'd first shown up on his doorstep, disheveled and depressed, he'd assumed it had something to do with my family, like last time.

"You don't know her, Meno, she's...she's unbelievable," I tell him.

"Wow. Jack Morrison losing his shit over a girl. Who would've thought?"

I lean back into the soft cushion of the couch and look over at Meno. He's sitting across from me in one of those bizarrely comfortable circular chairs, his feet on the coffee table between us.

"I'm crazy about her," I say softly.

Meno shakes his head. "This is not like you, Jack. How the hell did this happen?"

"I wanted her the minute I met her," I admit. As

soon as Candie had walked into my office and I got a good look at her perfect body, her sweet face, and her killer legs, I'd been hooked.

"You wanted to *sleep with her*," Meno points out.

"Without a doubt. And to be honest, for a minute there I thought maybe someone was playing a joke on me. Lily Kincaid and Robert Gleason's daughter as a corporate lawyer for my family's company. It didn't compute. And she was so stiff and awkward. The entire thing was bizarre."

"And when you realized she was serious? That she actually worked for the company?"

"I figured I'd play with her, like I had with that douchebag Kent. So I set up the press conference ambush. And then she got pissed at me."

Meno laughs. "And let me guess, it turned you on."

"It was more like…I saw another side to her. This raw emotion came out of her. She was so pissed, and it was written all over her face."

"So?"

"It's like this: when Trisha gets pissed at me when she's trying to help me with my computer, she takes a deep breath and you can see her controlling her anger. Or when Nancy is pissed at me, it's no surprise because her heart is always on her sleeve, and she's pissed at me like ninety percent of the time anyway. But with Candie, she has this big façade she wears on her face, in her posture, everything. Then when she explodes. Damn." I run my hand across the back of my neck. "Seeing her like that, it made me want to know who she *really* was."

"She became a challenge," he suggests.

"Definitely," I confess. "So I tried to crack open

the nut to find the woman inside the corporate lawyer."

"And what did you find?"

"A compassionate, emotional, caring person who is just as confused about where her life is heading as I was when I showed up on your doorstep last time. I got completely caught up in her. I wanted to know everything about her. But I had to give a little to get her to open up to me. So I ended up telling her things, things nobody but you know about me. I ended up exposing myself to her in a way I've never done before. And little by little, she showed me who she was."

"And then you decided to seduce her?"

"Seduction is not the right word. It was more like *begging*. When I first kissed her on the couch in my apartment, I thought maybe she'd slap my face. I would have deserved it. I had no business coming on to her like that, risking her career. But her reaction...Jesus."

"But I thought you said she pushed you away," Meno points out.

"Yeah, but before that...it was like fire. And then, yeah, she pushed me away. And I knew I'd been wrong. Candie is not the type of woman to ever sleep with someone she considers a client and definitely not with the likes of me."

"I'd like to meet this girl," he says. I just sigh in response, knowing he might never get the chance. "So, when you kissed her, she pushed you away. Then you tried again at the park?"

"That wasn't my intention. I knew I should just stop. I cared about her, and it wasn't fair to try to push her into ruining her career, even though *I* didn't think it was an issue. I felt sure my father wouldn't get worked up about it."

"But she worried about it."

"Yes. And the next time I saw her, I planned to apologize for kissing her in my apartment and suggest some way we could be friends, or at least work together cordially from then on or something. I spent all that night thinking about her, and all through brunch with my family the next morning. Then I found myself crossing the Bay Bridge almost without thought."

"So you called her and asked her to go for a walk in the park. And you're telling me your intentions were good at that point?"

"They were. I swear. I just wanted to talk it through with her. I mean, I knew it would be awkward as hell talking about our attraction to each other. People just don't talk about that stuff. But I felt like it was the right thing to do. But then, when we were there alone in the woods…the way she looked at me. It was killing me."

"And you went right back to begging?"

"Pretty much. So, I asked her take me back to her place. I wanted to give her the room to put a stop to all this if that's really what she felt she had to do."

"But she didn't."

"No."

"Well, obviously, some shit went seriously wrong after that or you wouldn't be here with me," he says, rising from his chair and heading to the kitchen.

He pulls two beers out of the refrigerator and pops the tops. He's right, of course. Two weeks after that beautiful Sunday, things had gone horribly wrong. I'd panicked, and my first reaction had been to book the next flight to Rio.

"Can't a guy come visit his friend once in a

while?" I say sardonically. We both know why I'm here, we've just completely avoided the topic until tonight.

Meno turns around, one beer in each hand, and heads back toward me. "Oh, yeah, just hop a plane to Rio because you miss my charm and my good looks." He hands me a bottle. "You're running, Jack. Just like before."

"Yeah, I am," I admit. There's no point in denying it. "And just like before, I need to cocoon here for a while so you can turn me into a butterfly."

Meno wasn't any Zen master or psychology guru, though there had been speculation that I'd seen both during my absent years. He was just my friend, my kinda crazy friend. The thing Meno did best was listen. When I hid out here before, he'd waited, then I'd talked and he'd listened. Eventually, I'd figured out my shit all on my own, just by talking it through with Meno. It's what I hoped to do this time, only faster. Because I've just spent six days away from Candie, and I am already miserable.

Meno tips his head back, laughing. "All right." He settles back into the chair across from me. "If I'm supposed to work my magic, you gotta tell me everything. So, pick up where you left off in the story. You got her alone in her apartment and made it to second base. What happened next?"

****

Three weeks ago—Berkeley

"I want more, Jack...more," she moaned.

I slipped my finger out of her. "Condom, sweetheart."

"Um...there's one in the drawer of the bedside

table."

I reached behind me and tugged on the little metal handle. Then I fumbled blindly in the drawer until my fingers landed on a square foil packet. I ripped it open and pushed the condom on quickly.

Candie watched me, biting her lip. Then she moved my hand and took hold of me. I moaned.

She stroked me up and down. "It's big," she said quietly.

Damn. This beautiful, sensual woman was even more inexperienced than I'd realized. I rolled her over so she lay on top of me. She moved her hand away to balance herself.

I placed my own hands on her hips and slid her down my body slowly, until I was inching my way inside her. She sucked in her breath, and I watched her face as I entered her. Then, when I was completely buried, she moaned. I cupped her head with my hand and pulled her to me for a kiss.

She attacked my mouth and started to move, slowly, eloquently. My hands were roaming all over her smooth skin. She was perfect. My left hand landed on her stomach. It was just a little soft, and I absolutely loved it.

She pulled her face back and looked at me. "Don't touch that. It's chubby."

"That is ridiculous," I said, stroking her belly while at the same time giving her gorgeous ass a squeeze.

She moaned again, and I thrust my hips forward. She started to move faster then, pushing herself up, tucking her knees beside my hips. She threw her head back as she pumped on top of me. She was so stunningly beautiful, it made concentration difficult.

My body tingled all over, and I failed to pay attention to the warning signs as I watched her. Until I realized I was about to come.

I moved my hand between our bodies and gave her a little nudge. Then she came, at exactly the same time I did. We both cried out. Then, Candie slumped onto my chest.

I wrapped both of my arms around her and held her tightly. I didn't ever want to let go. She lay still for a long moment. Then she let out a heavy sigh, and I knew regret had taken over.

"Don't go just yet," I said softly. "It's done now. Let's just stay like this for a while."

Instead of protesting, she nuzzled down farther against my chest. I slipped out of her and, while still hanging onto her with one hand, took care of the condom with the other. Then I rolled us both over so we were facing one another.

"Blanket," she whispered.

I gently pulled the quilt down underneath us both and threw it on top of our naked bodies. Candie snuggled into it and up against my chest. I rested my chin on top of her head.

"Candie, I am so happy right now," I told her.

She sighed. "Me too…kind of."

"Look. I know you are going to say that it's immoral or unethical or something. But we could just keep this—what's between us—a secret for now. No one has to know."

"It's wrong, Jack. I should probably quit my job."

"You could ask for a different assignment," I suggested.

She pulled her head back and scooted up in bed to

look me in the eye. "I'm brand new. I don't have that kind of clout."

Even as she said it, she was stroking small circles on my shoulder. And I wanted to believe she didn't regret this.

"So, keep it a secret for now. Just for now. We'll figure it out later."

She looked at me long and hard before answering. "That's not like me."

I ran my thumb over her cheek. "You are hyperethical. I like that about you."

"Hmm. Is that all you like?"

I ran my hand along her side. "There are many, many things I like."

She smiled and kissed me. "Honestly, I don't care about my job right this minute, Jack. I want to stay here with you for a while. Then I want to get something to eat because I'm starving. Then..." She ran one hand over my chest and down my stomach. "I want to do it all over again."

"Good plan."

"But we have to leave my apartment because I have no food and that was my only condom."

"You only had one condom?"

She nodded and laughed at herself. "It came in a gift bag from a bachelorette party."

"We'll get you some food," I said, kissing the tip of her nose. "And we're buying a great big box of condoms."

****

We went to the store and filled up Candie's cupboards, her refrigerator, and her bedside table. I discovered she didn't cook as I watched her pile dozens of cardboard boxes of insta-food into the cart. So I bought a few fresh ingredients, and when we got back to her apartment, I cooked up a killer lasagna.

Candie sat on a stool at her kitchen island with a glass of wine and watched me. I thought about how much I was enjoying this. I'd never been one to get excited over the mundane. Cooking for a woman, sitting quietly and drinking wine, talking idly as we lounged around the house on a Sunday evening—these were not the activities that got me out of bed in the morning. With all the other girls I'd dated, I really only got revved up when we went out somewhere and did something. But with Candie, I was perfectly content doing these everyday activities with her.

Once the lasagna was in the oven, I leaned over the counter across from her. She smiled at me. I took a sip of her wine.

"I've never had a man cook dinner for me, other than my father."

"And clearly you don't cook for yourself."

She shrugged. "Never wanted to take the time."

"You *are* a busy lady."

"Hmm. I can't remember the last time I wasted away a Sunday like this."

"Wasted?" I tried to sound offended.

She leaned over the counter and gave me a quick kiss. "In the best possible way."

"Hmm," I grunted.

She took of sip of wine, examining me closely. "What is brunch with your family like?"

"Not anywhere near as pleasant as dinner with you."

"Come on, tell me."

"Okay, but tit for tat. I get the next question."

"Fair enough." She rested her chin on her hand. It was adorable.

"This is how brunch goes: My mom and Chelsea hug me and kiss me and fawn all over me. My dad tries to find ways to have a conversation with me that won't lead to an argument. And my brother glares at me like I'm the antichrist."

"And you? How do you behave?"

"I do my best to fulfill everyone's needs. I try to give Chelsea as much attention as I can, reassure my mom I won't disappear again, stay out of a fight with my dad, and ignore my brother. And that's it. Nothing more to tell. Now it's my turn. Tell me about your childhood, Candie. All of it. I want to know everything."

"Jeez, you're demanding."

"I am. Come on, baby. Spill." When I called her "baby" her face moved, just the tiniest bit. I wasn't sure if it was shock, pleasure, or a combination of the two. But whatever it was, I liked it.

"It was good. I had a happy childhood. I have no complaints. It was just me and my parents. They were like my best friends. I do have extended family, mostly in Washington, and we saw them every now and again. But my parents were my whole world. They took me camping, hiking, fishing—catch and release only, of course—we did a lot. They also knew about a million people, and we were always at these big parties. Kids running all over the field playing, adults cooking over an open fire. That kind of thing."

"Hmm. Sounds like my dream childhood."

"Yes, I guess it kind of was. I suppose growing up

was very different for you?"

"Oh, yeah. A childhood filled with cold and sterile dinner parties with fancy people, the occasional European vacation, or throwing around a football with Hayden in the backyard in a tie and trying not to get grass stains on my pants. It doesn't compare to a bunch of hippies' kids running free in a field somewhere."

"It was nice," she said, running her finger over her glass. "But I—perhaps stupidly—always wanted what you had growing up."

"Huh. Well, we can still trade."

She laughed. "We kind of are. I make a big salary working for your family, and you are squeaking by at a nonprofit and hanging out with friends of my parents."

I grinned. "I suppose so, huh."

"That picture in your den—the one of you and your family—where was that taken?"

I smiled. She'd been snooping. I liked that. It meant she was interested in my life. "We vacationed in France. We stayed at this great little chateau, and befriended the family next door. I think the mom in that family took the picture. They had one kid, Cherie. She was my age, and she was my best friend that summer."

"Just for the summer?" Candie asked.

I shrugged. "I had a lot of best friends growing up." I took another sip of her wine. "What about you? Did you have a best friend when you were a kid, or a group of friends, anything like that?"

"No. I hung out with the kids of the people my parents knew and played with them. But I didn't have a best friend until I met Grace my senior year in high school. She'd been kicked out of her fifth boarding school and only had one semester to go. So her parents had enrolled her in public school. We met and instantly became inseparable. Still are. She's on a cruise right now, and I miss her."

She took a sip of her wine. "Then in college I met Meg. She's the artist I was telling you about. She's amazing. She and I have nothing in common, and I have no idea what she sees in me. But I'm glad she sticks around."

"What happened to you to give you such low self-esteem?" I asked.

Her back straightened. "What? *I do not* have low self-esteem."

"Oh, really? How come you freaked out when I touched your stomach?" I reached over the counter and moved my hand down along her torso. She didn't pull away this time.

"Look, I've been sitting in front of a computer for the last several years. I know my tummy is a little...ample."

"It's perfect is what it is." I stood up and rounded the counter so I could kneel down in front of her. I lifted up her shirt and licked a path across her belly button.

She let out a long sigh. "You don't have to say things like that. I'll still sleep with you."

"Baby, this belly is hot as hell."

"I thought men liked flat stomachs."

"Men like what men like. Don't put us into some standard category. And *I* like this."

She chuckled, which made her belly move, and I gave it a little nip. I looked up at her. "And what about this business with Meg being too good for you?"

"That's not what I meant," she said, running a hand

through my hair as I continued to peck at her stomach with my lips and teeth. "I just know that I frustrate her sometimes. For example, when I was getting ready to go out on my date with Hayden—"

My entire body stilled. And she quit speaking. I stood up slowly and looked at her. "That's who your date was with last Saturday? Hayden?"

She bit her lip. "I was going to tell you."

"Tell me now," I demanded. I felt like I was on pins and needles all of a sudden.

"He asked me out, and I didn't see any reason to say no. But we'd just sat down to dinner when I had to leave to bail you out of jail."

"And?"

"And nothing. He drove me to the airport."

I had never been a jealous dude. Never. But the thought of my brother with Candie was making me crazy. "Did he kiss you?"

"No! Jack, you're overreacting. Nothing happened. And it won't. Okay?"

"Wait. Why is it okay for you go out with him, but you're all worried you'll get fired if anyone knows you're with me?"

"Because *he's* not directly tied to my supervision, and *you* are my client."

I took a step back, needing to calm myself down. "I *am not* your client."

She let out a deep breath. Then, without warning, a tear trickled down her cheek. What was this? Candie did not strike me as a crier. But as I watched a sob escape her chest, I realized this was one more surprise she had in store for me.

I pulled her off the barstool and into my arms.

"Hey, what's this?" I asked, stroking her hair. She buried her face in my chest. For a long moment, I just held her.

Eventually, she looked up at me, wiping the tears from her cheeks. "I'm sorry. I have this problem."

"Um...What kind of problem?"

"I cry too much. It's always been this way. But I don't ever cry at work or in front of strangers, and I just did it in front of you and that's embarrassing," she said, her words rushed.

"Hey, I shouldn't count as a stranger," I said gently.

She smiled at me. "No. You don't."

"Or work," I said sternly.

"You're right. I need to...shit. I don't know what I need to do, Jack. Because you *are* part of my job. A big part."

"Okay, let's just take it one step at a time, all right?"

She took a deep breath. "Yes. One step at a time."

"Let's just start with dinner," I suggested.

"Yes, and then I think you should spend the night."

Chapter 14

I drove into the city on Monday morning feeling on top of the world. Apparently, my amazing night with Candie was written all over my face because Nancy noticed as soon as I walked in.

"Do you have a new girlfriend?" she asked, following me toward my office, the very same enclosed office I'd led Candie to believe didn't exist.

I stopped to grab a cup of coffee in the break room, avoiding eye contact with her. "Why do you ask?"

"Because you're fucking glowing."

I cocked my brow at her, then continued the walk to my office. She followed me in and shut the door behind her. "Come on, Jack. Spill. There's a girl, isn't there?"

Nancy was the vice president of the organization and my right-hand woman. But she was also my closest friend in SF. I'd been the best man at her wedding last month when she'd married her partner, our technology manager, Trisha.

"Okay, so I spent the weekend with an incredible woman. So what? We probably have a busy day. What's on the schedule?"

Nancy folded her arms across her chest and glared at me. "No way. You're late to work, and you're glowing. I want to know who she is."

I sighed. "She lives in East Bay—that's why I'm

late—and I can't tell you who she is."

"What? What the hell is that?"

"We're keeping it on the down low."

"What the fuck, Jack? You're an adult. Adults don't need to have secret relationships."

I turned to my laptop and fired it up, trying to ignore her.

"Holy shit! It's that hot lawyer from the company, isn't it?"

I tried to keep my expression neutral, but apparently it didn't work because Nancy said, "Jack, you player, you! You're sleeping with your babysitter!"

I abandoned the computer and leaned back in my chair. "Look, she's worried about losing her job. And the whole thing is very, very new. So we're just going to keep it quiet for now."

Nancy sat down on the edge of my desk. "I have a better idea: ask her to work for us. We could use an attorney. With the fundraising we've been doing lately, we can afford someone like her, someone who is still early in her career. I checked up on her, you know. She has a great track record with her volunteer work."

"You checked up on her?" I asked, surprised.

"Sure. She's your company-assigned babysitter, Jack. Of course I looked into her. Having her in this office is like having a corporate spy on site. We have to be careful."

"You spent too many years working on political campaigns, Nancy. You've become paranoid. This isn't Watergate."

Nancy put her hands on her hips and glared at me. "You were completely paranoid about Kent. In fact, you checked into him yourself, and you were super-vigilant about what we said every time he was in the office."

"What's your point?"

"My point is, your attitude is completely different because she's a good-looking woman."

I supposed it would have been a bad idea to tell Nancy I'd shared my personal calendar with Candie. "I've gotten to know her, Nancy. There's a lot more to her than being a lawyer for the company. She's got a good heart."

"Based on my research, I agree. So ask her to work for us."

"I kind of already suggested it, and she didn't bite. Besides, we could only pay her half what the company pays."

"Yeah, but we have perks. She'd get to work with awesome people, feel good about her job at the end of the day, and no one would care that she's sleeping with the boss."

****

I called Candie around one that afternoon.

"Hi," she said in a sultry voice that made my stomach ripple.

"How's your day going?"

"Well, no one's asked me about you. So I haven't had to figure out what to say."

I chuckled. "Well, score one, I guess. They got you working on something besides harassing me?"

"Yes. I'm doing some research for another project."

"You can tell me about it over dinner tonight."

"Actually, I have to work late tonight. And you have a racquetball game scheduled with the deputy mayor."

"Damn. Give a woman your calendar, huh? How about tomorrow night?" I asked, already disappointed that I'd have to wait over twenty-four hours to see her.

"I have dinner with my parents tomorrow. Would you...um...would you like to come?"

"Absolutely."

"Yeah? Okay. I'll pick you up."

"What time?"

"I just put it on your calendar."

I laughed. "Okay. And Candie?"

"Yes?"

"Bring an overnight bag. Since your parents live on this side of the Bay, you might as well stay at my place."

"That *would* be practical," she agreed.

After I hung up the phone with Candie, I turned back to the document on my computer. We'd been working on it for over a month. Nancy and I had gathered up a team of enthusiastic volunteers and interns who'd tirelessly researched, written, edited, and rewritten the document, preparing it for submission.

This was our priority method for saving the Baldy building, to get it historic designation, preventing Hayden from tearing it down. I did, of course, have a Plan B and even a Plan C, but looking at the polished document, I felt confident we wouldn't need them. This was the culmination of the blood, sweat, and tears of people who led the way with their hearts, not their wallets.

I clicked the document closed and pulled up my email. But before looking at it, I turned in my chair and stared out the window for a moment. In the distance, I could see the building Morrison and Sons was housed in. It stood like a glass and steel sentinel nestled in the heart of the financial district. The top seven stories of that building were occupied by my family's company.

Right then, I knew that my little brother was in that building, probably sweating my historic designation submission, maybe making a Plan B of his own. My father most likely sat in his office, ignoring the Baldy situation and hoping that somehow Hayden and I would work it out amongst ourselves, without him getting involved. At this time of day, my mom would have just left after delivering a lunch that her housekeeper made. My uncle James was probably eating his portion of the lunch while sitting at his desk. An accountant who served as the company's CFO, he preferred to deal with numbers over people, and that included his own family. My sister, Chelsea, was on her way to the office after class. She was being groomed to take over, against her will, and it meant spending a few hours a week shadowing my dad. She usually texted me pictures and web links the entire time she was supposed to be paying attention to my dad, or whichever executive he had leading her around. And somewhere in there was Candie.

I'd been in a tenuous position since I returned to San Francisco. I'd chosen a path that put me in direct conflict with my family, but I still maintained a relationship with them. It was a tough spot, and one a lot of my colleagues did not understand. I'd walked that tightrope for the past two years because I thought it was the only option for me. And now I'd put myself into an even tighter corner by sleeping with the lawyer my dad had hired to keep an eye on me. But I just couldn't bring myself to regret it.

****

Dinner with Candie's parents went very well. They seemed almost as thrilled to meet me as I was to meet them.

In the car, on the way over to their house, I'd asked Candie if she'd told them about us. "Yes," she'd said. "I called them last night and told them. They would have figured it out anyway. My mom has sex radar."

Lily did indeed ask us about our "relationship" over dinner, looking for all the world like a cat with cream on her whiskers when she did it. Candie told her that it was new, going great, but complicated because of her job. I admired how open and honest she was with them. I did not have that kind of relationship with my parents.

When we got back to my apartment after dinner, I wanted to review our time with them. "Your parents seemed over the moon that we're together," I said as Candie nestled herself next to me on my couch.

"Yes." She let out a soft chuckle. "They've been wanting me to date an activist type for years. In fact, my mom is always trying to set me up."

"Really?"

"Yes. She brings home any random dirty kid she finds at a rally to introduce to me. Hell, if I hadn't told them I was bringing you over and the nature of our relationship, she probably would have had a hippie sitting at the table waiting for me."

I laughed so hard, I almost spilled the wine she was holding. "And how many of these dirty hippies did you actually go out with?"

She made a face. "None of them. They are not my

type."

"Huh. What about me?"

She set her wine glass down on the coffee table and reached her hands up to cup my face. "You're different, Jack."

I gave her a quick kiss because I just *had* to before turning the conversation on her. "So, what were the two guys you dated like?"

She moved her hands over my neck and shoulders and then rested them on my chest. "The first one I met my sophomore year in college. We dated for two years, right up until graduation. I liked him a lot. We got along."

"But you didn't love him?"

"I didn't look at him the way my mom looks at my dad."

"So, what happened?"

"He proposed at the barbecue my parents held right after graduation. I felt bad...but I said no. I was focused on going to law school, and I knew I wouldn't have time for a boyfriend, let alone a husband."

"And the next guy?"

She shrugged. "He was a fellow law student. We both just needed to release some tension. So we had a little sex. But neither of us had time for much else."

"And since then?"

"Nothing."

"Too busy for fun, huh?"

"Something like that." She turned in her seat. "What about you, Jack?"

"You wanna know about my past conquests?" I grinned.

"Yes. Start with the reporter."

"Reporter?"

"The woman who you clearly prompted to ask a specific question at the press conference where you ambushed me."

"Oh yeah. You think I slept with her?"

She nodded.

"I did," I conceded. "But that's not why she asked the question. She owed me a favor because I gave her an exclusive once."

"But you *did* sleep with her?"

"Once."

"Is that how you do it, Jack? Are you a one-night-stand guy?"

"Sometimes it lasts all weekend," I quipped. She frowned at me. So I thought I better elaborate. "Look, I admit that, while my entire life changed when I went to Rio, my relationship with women didn't. I've been a player since I turned sixteen." I ran a finger along her cheekbone slowly. She shivered. "But I only played with women who were of the same mindset. I'm no heartbreaker. I wanted to have fun, and so did they."

"And there were a lot of them?"

I let out a heavy breath. "Yes. Before Rio, in Rio, and a few after Rio as well. Though I've been pretty busy since I got back. I haven't had a lot of time for...uh...relationships."

"But they weren't really 'relationships,' were they, Jack?"

"No. I've never had a *real* relationship."

"Never?" she asked, clearly surprised.

I shook my head. "And I have no idea how to do it even. But I think I can figure this out. I think *we* can figure this out. Two mid-twenties relationship neophytes trying to bumble our way into each other's lives." I grinned at her.

But her frown persisted. "Why me, Jack?"

"Because you're different, Candie. And the way I feel about you is different."

"How do you know it will last? It's only Tuesday," she pointed out.

I nibbled on her ear. "And I can't wait until next Tuesday."

****

Wednesday was just as good as Tuesday. After work, Candie came to the office and we both headed back to my place, where we stayed holed up until the next morning, thoroughly enjoying each other.

But Thursday was a shitty day. That morning, as I watched Candie slip into her sexy-as-hell pencil skirt, she told me she had an appointment and I couldn't see her that night. Then, as soon as I got to the office, all hell broke loose. Rumor had it my brother had gotten his hands on a copy of the Baldy historic designation paperwork, probably from someone who worked in an official capacity. No doubt it was someone easily bought off by the kind of spare cash my brother had at his disposal.

My staff and board members were all upset and in a snit over the ethics violations that were implied, if in fact it was true. But I knew how things worked, and I wasn't surprised. I wasn't worried either. The paperwork was filed, and he would soon have the opportunity to see it legitimately anyway. Besides, there was nothing Hayden could do about it now.

On Friday morning, I drove the sixteen-passenger bus filled with excited young people and Nancy to our planned protest. I hadn't seen Candie in over twenty-four hours, and I wondered if that day's event was to be a test of what we had together. When she'd left my apartment on Thursday morning, she hadn't said a word about my planned protest of Grover and Company. But it was on my calendar. She definitely knew about it. And it was her job to try to stop me from doing things like this, things my father would consider reckless.

She'd told me my dad had made it explicitly clear that her main duty was to keep my focus off Grover, even if it meant turning up the heat on Morrison and Sons. I knew when I gave Candie access to my calendar, I gave her the means to put a wrench in all my operations, maybe even to take me down, ruin what I've worked for. But I'd done it anyway because I wanted her trust. Because I wanted *her*.

I parked in the public lot across the street from our demonstration site and gathered all the other volunteers as they tumbled out of cars, cabs, and the BART station. Then we all walked over together, a decent-sized crowd of nearly one hundred enthusiastic supporters.

As we crossed the street, I could see Candie standing on the sidewalk, leaned up against a lamppost, her arms crossed casually over her chest. I knew that I was about to find out if I'd made a major mistake when I gave her my calendar.

As hard as it was not to rush over to her right away, I took my time, pulling the signs out of the van, making sure everyone knew the terms of our permit, and giving instructions about remaining firmly on public land. Then I sauntered over to her.

"Somehow, I knew you'd be here," she said, a

smile playing on her lips.

"So." I looked around. "You appear to be alone."

"Of course, I am. In fact, as far as my coworkers know, right now I'm at a meeting with you at your office. If this all goes badly, I will say I showed up at your office and you weren't there, so I tracked you down." She cocked her head to the side. "You didn't think I'd tell anyone what was on your calendar, did you?"

"No. But my father can be very persuasive, and Garrity is a sneaky asshole."

She put her hand on my upper arm. "You trusted me. I wasn't going to throw that away."

I felt a weird flutter in my chest and leaned down, closer to her. "But you came here?"

"I figured, if you get arrested, the least I can do is try to negotiate your way out of it."

I smiled. "While I appreciate that, this protest is completely legal."

"Yes. But the DA may find a way around that."

"I'm not afraid of the DA."

"What are you afraid of, Jack?"

I leaned closer. "I'm afraid that you won't let me kiss you right now."

"Hmm. Well, I've been thinking I need to fess up anyway."

"Oh, yeah?"

"Yes. I don't plan to stop spending the night at your place. So, I think I need to tell Garrity about us. If he fires me, I'll deal with the consequences. If I'm lucky, he'll just give me a new assignment."

"Or maybe he'll leave you on the same assignment," I suggested. "After all, it's easier to keep tabs on me this way."

"True." She smiled and moved her lips closer to mine.

"Hey, Jack! Are you gonna make out all day, or are you going to get on this megaphone and get the protest going?" Nancy called.

I rolled my eyes and gave Candie a quick peck on the lips before running over to join Nancy.

"You're a pain in the ass, you know that," I told Nancy as I took the megaphone from her.

She looked at me sternly. "We have to talk."

"Now?"

She nodded.

"Fine."

I handed the megaphone off to Trisha and gave a few instructions before ducking around the corner with Nancy. "What's up?"

"You know, and I know, that Hayden got the historic designation papers from someone at the state office. But there's a rumor going around that Candie stole them."

"*What?*"

"Look, she's been to the office a few times now, and everyone knows you two are—"

"And how do they know that?" I accused.

"Jesus, Jack, are you crazy? It's obvious. You look at that woman like she's the freaking Queen of England."

"That's not anyone's business."

Nancy let out a deep sigh. "Look, your employees trust you. And if you tell them Candie is not the spy they think she is, they'll believe you. But right now, you've got the Hayden thing, plus the fact that she's here this morning. It all looks bad. Between Baldy and the threats from the DA over Grover, plus you getting hauled into jail in New York, people are on edge, Jack."

"Fine. We'll address it when we get back to the office," I told her. Then I headed back to my, apparently, highly paranoid people to start the demonstration.

****

"You wanna have our meeting now?" I asked Candie.

She looked over my shoulder at the van slowly filling up with people. "Okay, but only if you ride back to the office with me."

I chuckled at her and went to give Nancy the keys. Once we were alone in the car, I told her about Nancy's concerns.

"I don't blame them," Candie said, her mouth in a straight line, her eyes on the road. "And they aren't far off base. While I wasn't the one who gave Hayden the papers you filed, I *was* tasked with spying on you."

She'd just confirmed Hayden had the designation paperwork. In a small way, she'd just betrayed the company for me, and I appreciated that.

While it should have surprised me that she was asked to spy on me, it didn't. My father had created a monster when he'd told Garrity to assign a lawyer to me. Garrity did not have the pure intentions of a man hoping to keep his son out of jail. He would take advantage of the request to serve his own needs, or those of executives, like Hayden, who had no scruples about screwing me over. But my father remained clueless about it all.

"And *are* you spying on me?" I asked her.

"No. I'm not doing that…"

"So, help me put them at ease. Will you, baby?"

"I don't know, Jack. I mean, why?"

"What do you mean, why?"

"I work for the enemy. Why is it important that your staff not see me as the enemy? I mean…I am…kind of."

I took her free hand and put it to my lips, kissing her palm and each of her fingers. "They can see you're important to me. They…" How did I put this? "My doings concern them."

"What you mean, Jack, is they worry about you. You are their leader. They look up to you. And they feel protective of you."

"I guess so, yeah."

"And you want them to know you aren't sleeping with some two-faced traitor who is going to be the ruin of you."

"Something like that. We could just talk to them, together."

"I can't…"

She looked so sad and conflicted, I couldn't stand to force the issue anymore. When we got back to Homes Without Inc., I took Candie's hand and pulled her through the office until I came to the one private room in the back. I pulled her inside and closed the door.

Candie looked around at the meager office. I only had a small desk in there, most of the room was taken up with fluffy chairs and two small couches arranged in a circle. But the coup de grâce was the two large windows overlooking the city.

"What is this place?" she asked, confused.

"My office."

She turned to me, hands on her hips. "You lied to me! You said you didn't have an office."

"Not exactly. I *implied* I didn't have an office."

She shook her head, tutting at me. "Jack, sometimes I don't know where I stand with you."

I closed the distance between us and took her in my arms. "I'll tell you exactly where you stand." She looked at me. There was something in her eyes, something I couldn't determine. "I'm crazy about you, Candie. I want to spend every waking minute with you."

Instead of kissing me, as I thought she would, she buried her face in my chest and took several deep breaths. "I feel so messed up right now, Jack."

I stroked my hand from the bottom of her neck down her back. "Hey, it'll be okay." I knew she was still freaking out about her job, the rumors among my staff, all of it. I just wished I could make it better for her.

"I don't know...I don't know what to do," she said softly.

I cupped her chin in my hand and gently pulled her face up so she could see me. She looked close to tears again. I hated that. So I pulled her over to the couch and settled her next to me.

"Talk to me, Candie."

"It's work...and you...and the two things combined..."

"I thought you decided to tell Garrity about us. I was under the impression your mind was made up." I desperately hoped she wasn't changing her mind about *me*. I didn't want Candie to have to choose between me and her career. I needed to make that clear to her.

"It's more complicated than that." Her eyes were watery as she stared up at me. She looked so pained, it was making my chest ache.

"Tell me what's going on, and we'll figure it out together."

She stared into my eyes for a long time. "I'm so conflicted."

Now I panicked. She was feeling trapped, between me and her job. "Look, Candie, it doesn't have to be me or the company. I know it's complicated. I know you feel like you're caught between a rock and a hard place. And I don't want you to be. So here's the deal: let's just be together, you and me. You figure out whatever you need to do to keep your job. If you want to tell me about it, you can. If you want to leave me out of that part of your life, that's fine too. I just want what I can get. I want whatever part of your life you're willing to give me. Because, baby, I want to be with you. And I'm willing to make whatever compromise I have to."

"Jack, I think I might be falling for you," she whispered, just before kissing me.

I pulled her to me and opened my mouth to her. I wanted her so badly at that moment. I didn't care how complicated everything was. I didn't care that we were in my office with my whole staff just outside the door. I *needed* her.

She didn't protest when I pulled her onto my lap so she straddled me, her skirt riding up on her thighs, or when I pushed it all the way up to her hips. Instead, she buried her lips in my neck, kissing and licking as her hands made their way to the button on my jeans. I leaned back to give her access, then I helped her push them down past my knees.

"This is crazy," Candie breathed as she pulled her lips back to my mouth. "I've never done anything like this." She scooted forward so the only thing preventing me from being inside her was the thin silk of her panties.

"Baby, I don't have a condom in my office," I whispered, feeling like I was going to die from the confession.

"Okay, so there must be a solution to this," she said, breathing hard. "We're two intelligent adults. Surely we can figure this out."

I would have laughed if I hadn't thought the movement would cause some serious trouble. "I'm clean, baby. Got tested last month, and I haven't been with anyone but you since."

"Mine was last year, and as you know, there's been no one." She kissed along my jaw, sending shivers down my spine.

"Yeah, but then there's birth control."

"Hmm…I take the pill. That would work, right?"

Despite the situation, I couldn't hide my surprise. "What? Why?"

"I have irregular periods, if you must know. I take it for that. But, um, it works for birth control, too."

"That's the idea," I breathed, feeling intensely relieved.

She rested her forehead against mine, wiggled her silk panties against my skin and said, "So…"

I reached down and pulled her panties aside. "I can't get enough of you, Candie." Then, I slid inside her.

Candie threw her head back and let out a soft

moan. I kissed her exposed throat. "Have to be quiet, though, baby," I said as I thrust my hips and her breath hitched. "This is an old building. Thin walls."

"I am so glad you have your own office," she whispered.

I moved faster inside her, my breathing growing more rapid, my pulse thudding in my veins. "Tell me why," I whispered hoarsely. "Tell me why you're glad."

"Because this feels so good. *You* feel so good."

I put my hand on the back of her head and pulled her down to me. "Hell yes, it does," I said before kissing her.

I thrust into her until I knew we were both close to orgasm. Then Candie ripped her lips from mine and lowered her head to my shoulder. She bit down, sinking her teeth into me through the thin barrier of my T-shirt. Her body shuddered, and I knew she was coming. But she usually made a lot of noise when I made her come. So instead, she took it out on my shoulder. I didn't mind, not one bit. And the feel of her orgasm around me, raw, with nothing between us, completely set me off.

"Jesus, baby," I sighed as I came inside her.

We sat like that, joined for a long time. Eventually, the sounds of the office outside the door reached us. The sounds of feet padding on the laminate flooring, computers making notification sounds, and voices all reached us.

"There are so many people out there," Candie said.

"Twenty-six to be exact."

"Why is it they all of a sudden got so loud?"

"Beats the shit out of me. I'm pretty sure none of

them were out there a minute ago."

Candie pulled away from me, causing me to literally feel her loss, and we both got redressed. Then she sat next to me on the couch and ran her hands through my hair.

"What are you thinking about?" I asked.

"You need a haircut," she said, smiling.

"You don't like my devil-may-care style?"

She ran her hand from my forehead to my neck slowly, sifting my locks through her fingers. "No. Actually, I like it. Maybe even a little longer."

"It was very long in Rio."

"Really? How long?"

"Long enough for a ponytail. I have pictures. I'll show you when you come to my house tonight and let me cook you dinner."

"I probably have to work late, especially after being gone half the day."

"That's okay. It'll be a late dinner It's Friday night, we don't have to get up early tomorrow."

"Hmm. Good thing I keep a change of clothes in my trunk."

"You should keep a change of clothes in my closet. Then you won't have to iron them in the morning." I'd teased her about exactly that on Thursday morning as she'd studiously ironed the clothes she'd pulled out of her bag.

Candie raised an eyebrow. "Clothes in your closet. That's a big step for a player like you."

"Yes, it is," I said simply.

Candie looked at me for a long time, like she was deciding something. "Jack, I need to get something off my chest."

"Okay, what is it?"

"On Saturday night, when I made that phone call in your den. Do you remember?"

I remembered all right. It was just before I'd kissed her for the first time. I nodded.

"I called Hayden."

It was just like before when she mentioned my brother. Maybe it was worse. My body tensed as I waited to hear what came next.

"He'd asked me out, days before. We were supposed to meet at a restaurant that night. I called to tell him I couldn't make it."

I didn't say anything. I battled with the jealousy welling up in me. This was still new and exclusive to Candie. But there was no mistaking it. And knowing it was my brother after her made it so much worse.

When I didn't talk, she continued. "Honestly, I don't know why I didn't tell you sooner. But lately, it's been weighing on me. It doesn't mean anything. I'm not going to go on a date with Hayden now, obviously. But not telling you, it felt wrong."

"So, um, you were interested in Hayden at one point?" I asked.

She stroked my cheek. "I guess. I mean, he has a lot of the characteristics of a man I thought I wanted."

I nodded. "Yeah, I suppose he does. He's a rich suit. Charming, well-groomed, good-looking," I said, trying to sound light and casual but not quite pulling it off.

"Yes. Truthfully, Hayden has all the things that used to be on my list. I can't deny that, Jack."

"I have none of the things on the list, right?"

She shook her head. "Not true. You are definitely

good-looking. In fact, you are downright *hot*." She smiled at me. "But it doesn't matter because I threw the list out the window."

"Yeah?"

"Absolutely. The list is gone." She made a slashing motion with her hand.

"Because?" I prompted.

"Because." She kissed me lightly. "I found out— much to my surprise—that you are everything I want."

"Me, huh? That seems unlikely."

"It sure does."

Chapter 15

Saturday was an incredible day. Candie and I drove north and hung out on the beach. We talked about absolutely everything except her job. In fact, we avoided the subject of my family altogether, aside from when I asked her to come to Sunday brunch with me.

"I want to share what we have with my family," I told her. "I know it sounds weird because my relationship with them is a little...complicated. But this is important to me."

She bit her lip. "When I go, will my...race be an issue?"

I was shocked at the implication, pissed a little even. But I couldn't blame her for asking. She didn't know them the way I did. So I tried my best not to let any irritation show. "No. I swear. They aren't like that."

She smiled apologetically. "I promise as soon as I've told Garrity about us, I will go with you."

So, reluctantly, I left Candie's apartment alone on Sunday morning and headed over the bridge to my weekly obligation.

It was turning out to be the average family affair. My mother worked hard to make everyone happy. She floated around the house, trying to keep everyone cared for and the conversation safe and friendly. She hadn't been like that when I was growing up. She'd been full of fire. I remember her antagonizing my father at every chance she got, constantly challenging him. But then I'd left. And while I knew she still gave him a hard time in private, when we were all together, these days she wanted nothing more than to keep the peace. It had changed her entire demeanor, and I was to blame for that.

Chelsea and I were tight. We always had been. She was the one family member I saw outside of our regularly scheduled group events. We hung out pretty often. And we understood each other well enough that we communicated all through the meal without actually having to talk to each other, merely by exchanging glances.

My dad and I had a strange relationship. Everyone said from the outside looking in it was absolutely baffling. I'd brought Nancy and Trisha to Sunday brunch once, and they had both spent the next week trying to psychoanalyze my relationship with my father. But to us it was pretty simple. We behaved exactly the same as we always had. He tried to be my rock, give me everything *he* thought I needed to succeed. I challenged everything he did and said while simultaneously offering him an almost hero-worship respect. What had changed after I left is that we both weakened a little in our resolve. He struggled with his tough-love methods these days, and I softened my challenges.

To the outside world, we were two men on opposite sides of one line. We were in a battle over business and heart. We were at war. Neither my dad nor I saw it that way, though. We were a family struggling together to find the right path, one where everyone won.

My brother was a whole other story. Things had

been strained between us since we were kids. So, we spent the entire time trying not to argue, which basically meant not speaking to each other at all.

I was pretty surprised when Hayden followed me out to the patio after brunch. I went out there to clean the pool for my mom. When we were kids, my dad had given us chores. Mine had been to take care of the pool. Now that I was an adult, my mother liked to purposely cancel the appointments with the pool man so she needed me to help out with it.

She'd done exactly that this week. Even though I was anxious to get back to Candie, I humored her. I walked out and picked up the strainer. Hayden stood on the opposite side of the pool and watched me for a while, sipping on his coffee. When it became obvious Hayden wasn't going to speak first, I did. "What's up, little brother?" He hated it when I called him "little brother," which was precisely why I did it.

Hayden took a casual sip of his coffee before lowering the mug to respond. "Things are going great for me. Better than for you, I think."

He had no idea how well things were going for me. "Oh, yeah?"

"Jail in New York, Jack." He shook his head. "That had to suck."

"I hear I interrupted your date."

He looked much more alert suddenly. "Did your babysitter tell you that?"

"Yes." I squatted down and rummaged through the water testing kit, trying to keep my expression neutral so as not to give away my real feelings about this conversation.

"And?"

"And what?"

"What did she say about me?"

This sucked. I wanted nothing more than to tell Hayden that Candie was mine. But I couldn't say a word. I'd promised her I wouldn't say anything to my family until she got the chance to talk to Garrity about us. And yes, she was stalling, but I couldn't blame her. This was an unusual situation for sure.

"Nothing. I just know I wrecked your date by going to jail," I told him.

"Don't worry. I'll get another chance," he said, smirking.

I looked up at him, ready to break my promise and say something, but he'd turned away and headed back into the house. By the time I'd finished cleaning the pool and wandered back inside, Hayden was gone.

****

Candie wasn't surprised when I showed up on her doorstep Sunday afternoon. And she didn't argue when I drove her and a small suitcase into the city on Monday morning. She stayed at my place the next three nights and even let me take her out to eat on Wednesday after work.

During dinner, she told me Hayden had asked her out again. "He wanted me to go to dinner with him tonight. I told him I had plans." She looked around the restaurant nervously as if she was half expecting him to walk in and catch us sitting there. "Then, as he was walking out the door, I told him I was seeing someone. I figured if I just said I had plans it would invite another offer. So...so I told the truth."

"Did he ask you who you are seeing?"

"No. Surprisingly, he didn't."

"I wonder if that's because he already knows," I speculated.

"You think Hayden asked me out because he knows about us?"

I took a sip of water before answering. "No. I think the first time Hayden asked you out was because you are gorgeous and smart and he wanted you for himself. But yesterday...I don't know. I might have given myself away on Sunday."

"Jack..." She sighed.

"Sorry, baby. He was talking about you, and I just don't have a very good poker face. I never have."

"What's the deal between you two?" she asked.

I rubbed my hand along my thigh, the cotton of my jeans causing a tension-relieving friction against my palm. "Honestly, I don't really know. Hayden and I got along fine until Chelsea was born. Then things just got...unhappy. He was always jealous of her and competing with me. My mom said it was just middle-child syndrome and he'd outgrow it. But he didn't. He got worse. He was always trying to outdo me at everything. If I had a good run at track, he had to do better, sometimes nearly killing himself in the process. So, I quit competing with him. I let him win at everything. And that seemed to help. By the time I was in college, we settled into a more comfortable routine. If he wanted to outdo me, fine. I didn't care. If he wanted to date a girl I'd had fling with, whatever."

I stopped rubbing my leg and placed that hand over Candie's instead. "Then, after I came back from Rio, things got really bad."

"That doesn't make sense. I mean, you came back and made it clear you didn't want to run the company.

You took yourself out of his way."

"That's what I thought, too. But…it's like with the Baldy building project." When I mentioned the building, Candie's hand stiffened under mine. "He knew I planned to target that building for historic preservation. And my dad intended to give the project to someone in the company, probably Kent or some other douchebag who my dad wouldn't expect to succeed. But Hayden asked to head up that project. He wanted it. It's like he was asking me to fight him over it. But I won't. I've left Hayden out of every mention of the building."

"But if he brings it up in the press, he always mentions you," she pointed out.

I shrugged. "I don't want to fight with my brother. I'll do what I have to do to try and save the Baldy building. But I won't play dirty. Not with my own brother."

"Jack…I need to tell you something, but I don't know how," she said, her eyes glistening.

"About your job?"

She nodded, and a tear slipped down one cheek. I reached across the table and brushed the tear off with my thumb. "Tell me when you're ready. I'm not going to pressure you."

She nodded weakly.

"I do have something I want to tell *you*, though," I said.

"What's that?"

"I won't fight Hayden for Baldy or any other building. But I *will* fight him for you."

She smiled. "I don't think that will be necessary."

****

On Thursday, it was me who grabbed a change of clothes and drove with Candie back over the bridge. She'd told me about the class she taught once a week and let me sit in on it. I sat in the back watching her help people with their problems. She seemed so relaxed and happy as she discussed how to declare bankruptcy or fight for child custody. I could see the satisfaction in her eyes when one of her students explained how Candie had helped her navigate the legal system to get her insurance company to pay a claim.

When we got back to her place, I hesitantly broached the subject of her future. "Would you consider holding some classes in the city?" I asked her as she pulled off her heels and deposited them on the bedroom floor. "I know a lot of people who could use your help." I sat on the edge of the bed watching her.

"I would consider that."

"You were happy doing that today, Candie. I could tell."

"I really enjoy it. I enjoy other aspects of being a lawyer, too."

"But you're not happy at the company," I said, expressing what I suspected.

She sighed. "It's complicated. I'm not sure everything I do there is…right."

I'd had a feeling something like this was going on. She'd been so hesitant to talk about work. And when it did come up, she got highly emotional about it. I knew it was more than just her internal conflict about sleeping with me that was bothering her, and I suspected she was working on evictions and it was making her miserable.

"Maybe you should focus on the things you like to

do and take your career path in that direction instead," I suggested.

"Jack, I don't charge to hold those classes. There's a small fee the students pay to cover the room rental, and several of them have scholarships for that even. I can't make a living doing that."

I decided to plunge in with the job offer Nancy and I had discussed earlier in the week. "You could work for Homes Without Inc. We need a lawyer."

"I don't need a pity job, Jack."

"It's not," I said, getting up and walking over to my bag that was perched on the edge of her dresser. I took out my computer, sat back down on the bed, and pulled it open. Candie sat down beside me, a curious look on her face.

"I'll prove that I'm serious about this." I opened a folder on my desktop. "See, these are all the funds we raise money for," I said, pointing to a list of labeled folders nested within the fundraising folder. "They're for specific activities. Nancy and I have been very successful lately at fundraising. We want to use my trust fund as an endowment rather than bleed it dry and have the organization run out of money. As an endowment, it will continue to provide operating funds and secure the organization's financial future. Meanwhile, we raise money for the special projects we want to do." I turned to her. "I'm building a strong foundation here, Candie, not a fly-by-night operation."

"I can see that."

I moved the cursor up and down on the screen, drawing her attention to it. "This is the list of funds, and here it is, see, 'lawyer.' We've gotten donations from several lawyers and other donors. Enough to pay for two years' salary." I clicked open a file. "This is the pitch we've been using. It outlines what an on-staff lawyer would do for the organization. Things like file lawsuits on behalf of tenants, research and file for historic designations." I looked up at her. "Nancy and I did the one for the Baldy building with a team of college kids. I think we did all right, and I hope to find out if we succeeded sometime next month, but we could use someone who knows what the hell they're doing for future filings."

Candie made a strange face, a look I couldn't decipher. So I decided to continue with the list, hoping something else would catch her fancy. "It also involves teaching classes to people about navigating the legal system, how to fight eviction, how to assert tenants' rights, that kind of thing. And, of course, general legal counsel."

"Which is code for keeping you out of jail, right?"

"Pretty much, but this sounds better." I put the computer on the dresser and turned to face her. "What do you think? You like doing all those things, right? You would be perfect for this job, Candie. I know it doesn't pay great, but you could save expenses by living with me."

"You move fast, Jack."

"I can't seem to help it," I said, wrapping my arm around her waist. "You and me, this is...it's going places, I know it."

She stroked my cheek with one hand and bit her lip. "You know, when I got the job at Morrison, I thought it was all my dreams come true. A great job with good pay, better than I'd hoped so early in my career, good potential to move up in the company, prestige. It was everything I thought I wanted all through law school."

"But now?"

"I don't know anymore. The job…it's not what I thought…But I got you out of it."

I grinned and kissed her nose. "Yes, you did."

"Jack, I think you are the one person on the planet who can truly understand this. I thought I wanted to live a certain way for a long time, most of my life, really. And now, suddenly, I find myself questioning all that. I feel like I'm standing on the edge of a cliff, staring down, trying to figure out how to make myself jump. You know what I mean, don't you?"

Candie knew that I would understand because that's exactly what had happened to me when the thing with Delores went down. I'd had to rethink my entire existence. She'd just eloquently explained what that had felt like.

"I *do* understand."

"I need a little time to adjust to it all," she said softly.

I understood that, too. I just hoped that Candie's method of adjusting didn't require five years in Brazil, like mine had.

****

"What the hell are you doing here?"

"That's a nice way to greet your brother," I said to Hayden as I sat down in the leather chair across from his desk.

"Since when do you set foot in the evil empire? Did you have a meeting with Dad or something?"

"No. I came to see *you*." I folded my arms across my chest and internally chastised myself for coming here.

This was so stupid. My jealousy had led me to go to Morrison and Sons. This ridiculous male pride had welled up in me this morning as I watched Candie sleeping. It had made me want to tell Hayden to back off. I wanted to tell him she was mine. But technically, I couldn't, which made this whole thing pointless and ridiculous.

"If you wanna talk Baldy, I'm going to have to refer you to our legal department," he said, purposely flipping through a set of papers on his desk so he looked too busy and important to bother with the likes of me.

"Give me a break, Hayden. We both know that wouldn't go anywhere."

He met my gaze. "Then what do you want?"

"Can't I just come visit my little brother?"

His eyes narrowed.

"Let's talk."

"About what?"

"I don't know. Are you seeing anyone right now?"

"What the hell, Jack? You wanna make small talk now?"

I shrugged. "Why not?"

"Because you and I haven't made small talk in seven years, that's why."

"Maybe it's time we did. I'm seeing someone," I told him.

"When *aren't* you seeing someone?" he said dismissively.

I swung my feet up onto his desk and leaned back in the chair. "See, that shows you how little we know about each other these days. I haven't seen too many women since I got back. It's part of the new Jack."

Hayden scoffed. "Oh yeah, I suppose 'long-term' and 'monogamy' are not words that made it into the new Jack, though, eh?"

Hayden, despite his playboy reputation, had a habit of hanging onto one girlfriend for a while. "Serial monogamy" our dad always called it. And because of that, he felt justified in making fun of my flings and one-night stands. I supposed it was the one thing in which he felt morally superior to me.

"Actually, I'm very serious about this woman."

"Good for you, big brother. I'm thrilled for you. Did you come here just to tell me that?"

"How about you? You seeing anyone?" I asked again.

I knew I was pressing my luck. I also knew I was being a ridiculous ass. And I risked really pissing my girlfriend off. But I couldn't seem to help myself. Even if Candie had told Hayden she was seeing someone, I didn't trust him to back off. And if he suspected she was seeing me, it might make him that much more determined.

Hayden leaned forward, suspicion written all over his face. "What are you fishing for, Jack?"

"I'm bringing my babysitter to brunch on Sunday, and I want to know where you stand before I show up with her at Mom and Dad's house."

Hayden's eyes narrowed. "Why are you bringing Candace to brunch?"

I shrugged. "Kent's been to brunch. It's not unprecedented."

"Kent wasn't hot."

"Also, I hated Kent," I said, trying to look casual

and snarky. "Candace is easier to put up with."

I could see the suspicion in Hayden's eyes. So I tried to cover up a little. "To tell you the truth, I figure if I show Dad I'm getting along with her and cooperating, he'll back off."

Hayden leaned back and grinned. "Good luck with that, Jack. You're an even bigger disappointment to Dad than I am. Get used to it."

"Whatever. Hayden, are you stalking Candace or not? I just need to know the score before Sunday."

"Don't worry, I won't mack on your babysitter over cinnamon rolls at Mom's house."

I hadn't gotten what I came for, not that I was entirely sure what that was. And I couldn't do what I really wanted to: tell my brother that Candie came home with me every night and he needed to back off. But there wasn't much else I *could* do. So I swung my feet off the desk and stood up.

"You're a peach, Hayden." I walked to the door. "See you on Sunday."

With no little trepidation, I took the stairs down two floors and walked straight to Candie's office.

"Mr. Morrison," Candie's secretary, Janice, said cheerfully. "What a pleasant surprise."

"Hi, Janice. I haven't seen you since you had a much shittier boss," I said, referring to when she worked for Kent.

Janice stifled a laugh with her hand, and her eyes twinkled at me. And right then, that's when I remembered I'd once made out with Janice in the stairwell of my office. Damn. This was not good.

"Um, is Candace in?"

Janice moved around her desk so she stood right in

front of me. "Yes. She's in her office. But, um, I haven't had lunch yet, and…"

That's when the door opened. I glanced up to see Candie standing in the doorway of her office at the exact same moment Janice put her palm on my chest.

"Candace," I said, taking a step back from Janice.

Janice seemed to remember herself and moved away from me as well.

Candie smirked. "Jack. Interesting to find you *here*."

"Do you have a minute?" I asked, walking toward her.

"Sure." She extended her arm toward her office.

I followed her in. Candie had an amused look on her face as she closed the door behind her.

"I can explain."

"I bet I can guess," she said, folding her arms across her chest. "You slept with my secretary, didn't you, Jack?"

"Technically, no. We made out in a stairwell while her boss talked on the phone in the lobby. And then she had to go and take a cab back to Morrison with him, so…"

"You didn't have time for the actual sex," she guessed.

I leaned back against her desk, the heels of my hands resting on the varnished surface. "I suppose that's what it amounts to, yes."

She shook her head. "Such a player, Jack."

"I *was*. I'm a changed man now."

"Just like that?"

I snapped my fingers. "Just like that."

Candie took a few steps toward me. "What are you

doing here? You miss me?"

"Yes. But I actually came to get my alpha male on."

Candie's face showed panic. "Oh no! You came to confront Hayden, didn't you?"

"Yep." I reached out and wrapped a hand around her waist, tugging her toward me. "I was having a serious testosterone-laden moment."

Candie rested her hands on my shoulders. "Not a good look, Jack."

"No?"

"I am not a prize to be won."

"No, you're not," I agreed.

"So, what happened?"

"Nothing really. I mean, I couldn't actually tell him about us. So I ended up just being an ass."

"Hmm."

"You're thinking about dumping me right now, aren't you?" I teased.

"Hmm."

"Admit it. You're realizing I'm not worthy of your affection."

Candie ran her finger over my lower lip. "I don't know. Even if you aren't, I might have to make an exception."

"Thank God," I said, cupping my hand behind her head and pulling her lips to mine for a kiss.

She let me kiss her for a minute, then pulled back and rested her forehead against mine. "What have you done to me, Jack? It's like all my ethics have gone out the window. Here I am kissing you *in my office*."

"That's nothing compared to what happened in *my office* last week," I reminded her.

"You're not helping."

"Sorry."

"I feel like...I'm just not the same person I used to be."

"In a good way or a bad way?" I asked, feeling nervous about her answer.

"A little of each I suppose."

"Hmmm." I wasn't happy with that.

"But," she said, raising her head to look me in the eye, "I'm a hell of a lot happier."

Chapter 16

Candie looked amazing. We were walking through the park on a perfect San Francisco day. She wore a pair of sunglasses, yoga pants, a tight cotton shirt, and a black leather jacket. She didn't look like a corporate lawyer as we walked through the park that Saturday morning. She looked like my girlfriend.

"I have something to tell you," she said, stopping on the path in front of a concrete bench.

"Okay."

"I quit my job yesterday. I gave my two week's notice."

I was in shock, and all that came out of my mouth was, "What?"

She looked past me for a second. "Maybe we should sit down." She pulled me over to the bench. "I intended to tell you last night, but you distracted me."

That was unfair. She was the one who'd been walking around my apartment in leggings and a tank top. We were lucky I'd managed to get dinner cooked.

"Wow! I mean, I'd be lying if I said I wasn't happy about this. But are you okay?"

"Yes. I mean, I'm a little freaked out about making my rent and my car payment at the moment. So I'm hoping your job offer still stands."

Everything was happening much faster than I'd anticipated. But I didn't mind. Once I knew what I wanted, I went after it. I'd been that way with my mission for Homes Without Inc., and I was proceeding that way with Candie. I didn't see any reason to stop. So I told her, "Of course, it does. And don't worry about the rent. You can move in with me."

"Jack, we've been together for two weeks."

"Don't care. This is a long-term thing, Candie. I know it." She looked at me, her eyebrows scrunched up. I thought I better change the subject and try this again later. I might be ready, but Candie wasn't. She was a far more cautious person than I was, and I'd already pushed her far out of her comfort zone. "What did Garrity say?" I asked.

She shrugged. "I left my letter of resignation on his desk at the end of the day." She kissed my cheek. "You look happy."

"I can't lie. I am." I threw my arm around her and pulled her to me. "And you're going to be just fine, Candie."

"Yes. I am. And my parents will be thrilled."

"Speaking of parents. Would you be interested in going to Sunday brunch with me tomorrow?"

"Yes. I would like to go. But…it might be kind of awkward since I just quit my job."

"Maybe. But we have to deal with it at some point. Better to get it over with, yeah?"

"You're right. And I did promise to go with you as soon as I told Garrity about us." She bit her lip. "Of course, I didn't actually tell him about us. I just resigned."

"Same thing." I leaned in to kiss her when I was interrupted by my phone ringing. I fished it out of my pocket and looked at the screen. "It's Nancy. I forgot to tell you. She and Trisha want to invite us to dinner next week." I hit ignore, then texted Nancy that I was asking Candie about dinner right that minute.

"Nancy's your best friend. She's important to you. I'd love to get to know her and Trisha better."

"Okay. I'll tell her to sign us up."

"I'll put it in your calendar," she teased.

"I'm anxious for you to meet Chelsea, too. I thought about inviting her over tonight so you could meet her without the rest of the family. But she's busy."

"I wish I could introduce you to Grace. But she's on a damn boat in the middle of the Pacific right now. But Meg! You could meet Meg! I'm going to call her right now to see if she can meet up with us for lunch. We could walk down to that Korean place; she doesn't live far from there."

"Sounds perfect."

"She's going to love you. For the first time ever, I'm dating someone Meg will approve of."

"What about Grace? Will she love me, too?"

Candie's mouth turned up on one side. "I don't know. You might not make enough money for Grace."

"Hmm. So the trust fund doesn't count?"

"We could probably spin it."

She pulled her phone out of her purse, but I took her hand in mine, stopping her from making the call. "I want to tell you something."

She smiled. "You do, huh?"

"I know we've only known each other for a month. I know that your life has been turned upside down in that short period of time. And now I want you to work with me and live with me. And I guess I just wanted you to know how very real this is."

She swallowed hard. "It is all very, very real."

"But…you're okay with it?"

She took a deep breath and let it out slowly. Then she said, "I admit we're moving fast. It's outside my comfort zone, and probably yours as well. But I think we should go with it. Whatever this is, it's swept us up." She shrugged. "And I can't really fight it."

I was so happy, I felt like nothing could pop my bubble. "Yeah?"

"Jack," she said softly. "I look at you the same way my mom looks at my dad. I can't deny it, and I can't delay it until an appropriate amount of time has passed. It is what it is."

I wanted to kiss her. But we were in the middle of the park. I could hear kids playing nearby. And one kiss was not going to do it for me. So I bit my lip and stood up, holding my hand out to her. "Come on. We need to hightail it back to the apartment. You can call Meg on the way."

****

Candie looked nervous as we approached the imposing double wooden doors to the Morrison mansion, a place I had once called home. I rubbed her lower back gently with my left hand while opening the door with my right.

We were greeted by Delia, my parents' newest housekeeper. She'd only started a few weeks ago, having replaced Sonya, who'd finally retired after cooking, cleaning, and chasing after kids for twenty-five years.

Delia and I spoke in Portuguese for a few minutes. I was conscious I might be making Candie uncomfortable. So I stopped and turned to her. "Sorry, I learned quite a bit of Portuguese in Rio, and while Delia is a native Spanish speaker, she knows enough for us to get by."

To my great surprise and delight, Candie turned to Delia and said, "*Me llama* Candace. *Mucho gusto*, Delia."

"*Mucho gusto!*" Delia squealed, pulling Candie into a hug.

"Oh, come on you guys. *Estoy oxidada*," Chelsea said, walking into the foyer. "You're making me look *malo*."

I looked Chelsea over quickly. Her short brown hair was tucked behind her ears, making her glasses seem even larger than usual. A blouse that was way too big for her draped over her thin frame, and her jeans hung precariously on her hips. She looked nothing like the heiress to a massive family fortune. And she was perfect.

"Come here, little sister," I said, pulling her into a hug. I did this every time I saw her. Because every time I saw Chelsea, it made me happy.

Chelsea accepted my squeeze but pulled back quickly so she could turn to face Candie. She looked her up and down slowly. "Wow. She's a freaking beauty queen, Jack."

"Way to make her feel comfortable, Chels," I said, ruffling the frizzy curls on top of Chelsea's head.

Chelsea pushed my hand away and extended hers to Candie. "It is so nice to meet you."

"You too, Chelsea. I've heard a lot about you."

"Oh yeah?" Chelsea looked between Candie and me, her eyes narrowing. "Seems like you're pretty close with your babysitter, Jack."

I diverted her. "Did you tell Dad about your class load this semester?"

She sighed. "I did."

"Oh yeah? Good for you." I turned to Candie. "My little sister is nearly as much of a rebel as me. She changed her major from business to media studies." I looked at Chelsea. "Had to piss Dad off."

"He thinks it's a phase." She grinned.

We both knew it wasn't. Chelsea had been behind a camera since she was a toddler. She was going to be a filmmaker someday, and I was proud as shit of her.

"Where are all my children?" I heard my mother call.

"Come on. We should go in," Chelsea said conspiratorially. "Something tells me, whatever you're going to do today will take some heat off me." She grabbed my hand and pulled me toward the living room. Candie followed behind us, and Delia disappeared.

"Jack!" my mom exclaimed as if she hadn't seen me in years.

"Hi, Mom." I gave her a quick hug and turned to Candie, taking her hand. "Have you met Candace Gleason yet?"

My mom, who was shorter than a ten-year-old boy, looked at my hand linked to Candie's. When she shifted her head to look up at Candie, the perfectly dyed blonde hair not moving an inch, there was a definite twinkle in her eye.

"You know, I haven't." My mom extended her hand, and Candie took it with her free one. "But I've heard about you. You are the young, hotshot lawyer John hired."

"I don't know about hotshot," Candie said modestly. "But I am the newest, ma'am."

"Call me Frances," my mom said casually.

"Thank you…Frances," Candie said quietly. I gave her hand a little squeeze.

"How do you know Jack?" my mom asked.

"I assigned her to keep an eye on him." We all looked up to see my father emerge from the hallway. He walked over and clapped me on the back. "Hi, Son."

Before I went to Rio, a lot of people said I looked like my dad. Then, after I got back, I never heard that again. The truth was I'd inherited his features. We were about the same height with the same nose and cheeks. I most definitely had my mother's eyes, but aside from that there was no mistaking I was my dad's son. The difference was he always looked composed and professional, even while sitting in the living room at six in the morning on a Sunday wrapped in a bathrobe with a cup of coffee on his knee. And since I'd returned from Brazil, I always appeared laid-back and slightly unkempt. Some people claimed I had a look in my eyes like I might do something off the wall and unexpected at any time.

"John," my mom said sternly, directing her critical gaze toward my father. "What do you mean by 'keep an eye on him'?"

"Oh, come on, Frannie. You know about this. I've had a lawyer assigned to Jack for the last two years."

My mom pursed her lips.

"Mom, don't you remember that douche—um, Kent guy," I reminded her.

"I thought he was supposed to help Jack," my mom said, still focused on my father.

"He was supposed to get in my way," I told her.

"No, he was supposed to keep you out of jail," my dad said lightheartedly. "And now that's Candie's job."

Not only had my dad paid absolutely no attention to the fact that I stood in the middle of the living room holding Candie's hand, but he obviously didn't know she'd quit yet, either. This could make things more awkward than I had anticipated.

Meanwhile, his statement seemed to really darken my mom's mood. She didn't like talking about me going to jail or anywhere else for that matter. "Oh, Jack," she said, turning back toward me and frowning.

"Don't worry, Mom. I haven't been to jail in—" I had been about to say six months. But then I remembered. "Oh, wait…"

"Three weeks," Candie finished for me.

"A jail in New York," my mom said, pursing her lips together. "I can't even imagine," she shuddered.

I pulled my hand out of Candie's and clapped loudly. "Okay, change of subject. I'm starving. Let's eat."

"Delia says it's ready, but I don't know where the hell your brother is," my dad said. "He showed up an hour ago."

"He went for a swim," my mom told him. She turned to my sister, who lingered at the edge of the room. "Chelsea, will you go get Hayden?"

"No need. I'm right here." Hayden walked through the sliding glass door that connected the living room to the pool area. He wore just a pair of swim trunks with a towel draped over his shoulders.

"Hayden, you're dripping everywhere," my mom scolded.

My brother was a pretty good-looking guy, and he was fairly ripped because he spent a ridiculous amount of time working out. And I knew he'd planned this on purpose. He wanted Candie to see as much of him as possible. I rolled my eyes at him. He winked.

"Hi, Candace," he said congenially.

"Hello, Hayden," she returned stiffly.

"Go put a shirt on," I snapped, and grabbed Candie's hand again to escort her to the dining room.

We sat around the massive rectangular table, Candie right beside me. Delia brought out the food, and I chatted with her in Portuguese while my mother smiled, my father looked bored, and my brother stared—practically drooling—at my girlfriend.

We made a lot of small talk for the first part of brunch, discussing the weather, the upcoming parades and events in the city, that kind of thing. And I knew Candie was nervous about telling my parents about us and about telling my dad she'd quit. She sat quiet and stiff beside me, and I wanted to help her out. So I thought I'd get it over with.

About twenty minutes into the meal, I broke the news. "So, um…I have something to tell you guys," I said, setting down my fork and leaning back in my chair. I took Candie's hand and held it on my lap. "Candace and I are dating."

A deep silence engulfed the table for a moment. Not wanting to know what my brother thought about this, I ignored Hayden and focused on my dad. He looked deep in thought, not pissed, just contemplative.

Then my sister broke the silence. "I knew it!"

I winked at Chelsea, then turned back to my dad.

"How long has this been going on?" my mom

asked, a smile lighting up her face.

"Two weeks. But it's serious. Very serious," I said, squeezing Candie's hand. "I asked her to move in with me."

"Seriously? After a couple of weeks? Damn, Jack," Chelsea said.

"I want you to know, Mr. Morrison," Candie said, looking at my dad. "I gave my notice to Tom Garrity yesterday. I know it was wrong to wait this long, but—"

My dad held his hand up. "Don't apologize for anything, Candace." His gaze shifted to me. "Jack, you look happy. Maybe settled even."

I nodded.

My dad leaned back in his chair, looking relaxed. "Then, congratulations. I couldn't be happier."

"Dad! He seduced his babysitter," Hayden said. I finally looked at him. The petulant middle child was back with a vengeance. His blue eyes, so much like mine, were on fire. His hands were placed on the table, palms spread, his fingers pressing into the wood. And the vein in his neck, which I always watched with amusement when he got upset, pulsed.

My dad shrugged, effectively blowing Hayden off. He turned to Candie and pierced her with his gaze. "The thing is, I think you have a lot of potential, Candace. I hate to see you go. Any way I can change your mind about quitting?"

"I'm afraid not, sir. But I'm glad you aren't angry with me."

"What are you going to do? I'm not losing you to a competitor, am I? Grover?"

"She's going to work for me," I told him.

My dad chuckled. "Figures."

"It's too bad," Hayden said. He looked much more relaxed all of a sudden. And a red flag went up in my head. He was up to something. I held my breath as he said, "Candace did some good work in the short time she was with us."

I let my breath out.

"She did," my dad concurred.

"Like the Baldy project," Hayden said.

And there it was. My body tensed up at the exact same moment Candie's hand turned to ice in my palm.

"If it hadn't been for Candace," Hayden continued, "we wouldn't have found all the flaws in Jack's application for historic status."

It was like the world was moving in slow motion. I turned to look at Hayden, my eyes stabbing him with a glare so intense I was sure it traveled on the air between us. "Flaws?"

Hayden shrugged casually. "It was little things, you know—a wrong date here, a misspelled name there. But it was enough to stall out the application." He gestured to Candie. "And she's the one who found it all."

Slowly, so slowly, it felt surreal, I turned my entire body toward Candie. She watched me, a look of absolute horror on her face.

My brain wasn't functioning. But I could feel my heart. It was broken. I'd been betrayed.

Without any conscious thought, I dropped Candie's hand and rose from my seat. The chair tipped back and fell on the marble floor with a deep clap. I stepped around it and stalked through the archway, into the living room, and toward the foyer. My family called to me, but I paid no attention. Precious silence greeted me as I slammed the front door behind me and jogged along the circle drive, past Candie's car and out onto the street to hail a cab.

****

Present day—Rio

"Wow," Meno says as I finish my story.

I take the last swig of my beer and pick at the label. "Yeah."

"So you were pissed. You jumped on a plane and came here, then kept your mouth shut about the whole thing for a freaking week."

"Yep."

"So, are you still pissed?"

"I stopped being pissed at Candie about fifteen minutes into the flight. I imagined how awful that whole situation must have been for her. She's very ethical. And then she slept with me. It went against everything she believes in. On top of that, she had my calendar. She knew my every move, but she didn't tell anyone at work. And that was technically her job. And then my jackass brother gave her an assignment he *knew* would force her to work against me."

"But she didn't tell you," Meno points out.

"She tried. I thought she was working on evictions and needed time to process her role in kicking people out onto the street. I told her she didn't need to tell me what was going on at work. I figured talking to me about it right then would only make her feel guiltier. I thought I could help her through it better after she'd left the company. But the whole time, the truth was eating her up. I think Hayden knew about us. I don't know how, but he did. And he sabotaged the whole thing."

"So you're pissed at *him*?"

I run my hand through my hair. "I was for a

175

minute. Now I'm just pissed at myself."

"For running again?"

"Yes."

"Do you still feel betrayed?"

I look at Meno. He's lounging across his chair, one arm flopped over the top of his head, gazing at me with concern. This man is a true friend. I don't know where I'd be without him.

"I don't think so. I get that she had to do what she had to do. And honestly, if she didn't mean anything to me, I would have laughed the whole thing off, called my brother a prick, and went on with my life. I'll find another way to save that building." I let out a deep breath. "But I didn't do that. My world basically came down around my shoulders at that damn table in my parents' dining room. And so I ran."

"And that," Meno says, pointing his finger at me, "is because you're in love with her, isn't it?"

I nod. "Yep."

"Damn, man. What are you going to do now?"

"This afternoon I used your computer to book a flight. I'm headed out on Tuesday morning."

"Well, I guess that gives us a couple days to figure out what the hell you're going to say to get your girl back."

"We're going to need more beer."

Chapter 17

Present day—Berkeley
Candace

"Damn, girl. That's quite a story," Grace says, rubbing her hands along the jeans material at her thighs.

It reminds me of something Jack does when we're having a serious conversation. Another stupid tear slips from my eye.

"Okay…" She leans forward. "So, what are we going to do about it?"

"Do? What do you mean? What can I do?"

"Look, Candace, you've been rotting in this apartment for a week. Have you even gone to work?"

I bite my lip and confess. "No. I called in sick all week."

"And have you tried to call Jack?"

I shake my head and that damn tear flies into my hair.

"So, let's go find him."

"And say what exactly? Hi, Jack. Sorry I betrayed you. Will you please take me back?"

"That's a good start."

I roll my eyes at her.

"Remember when I got drunk and kissed that guy at the piano bar? I told Eric everything. I confessed. I apologized. And I asked him to trust me again. And he did. He does."

"Grace, that was a drunken kiss at your bachelorette party. I *betrayed* Jack. I screwed him over. I sabotaged everything he has been working toward for the past two years! Do you know how much money he sank into that project? How many lives will be affected when they tear that building down?"

"Okay, but you can fix that, right?"

"Seriously?"

"You are Candace Gleason. Can you fix it or not?"

I think about that for a moment. "You know. Maybe I could. I could refile for the historic designation. I could fix all the mistakes I found and—"

"Great." Grace stands up. "We'll do that later. First, we need to find Jack."

I look up at her. "How?"

"We'll start with his apartment. Do you have a key?"

I nod. "You want to break into Jack's apartment?"

"Unless he opens the door, smiles, and pulls you into his arms, yeah."

Grace manages to get me into her car, and we make our way to the city. I'm practically shaking as I watch her hit the buzzer. When Grace tries with no answer for a few minutes, she demands I tell her the code and opens the front door with it. I follow her listlessly as she heads to the elevators and asks me what floor Jack's apartment is on.

I have been living in a deep well of self-pity for the past week. When I wasn't feeling sorry for myself or being angry at myself, I reveled in how quickly I had fallen madly in love with Jack.

I guess I'd always thought falling in love was this

slow, gradual process that took place over months or years. I thought a person knew it was happening to them and rode it like a wave. That's not how it had been for me. I had fallen fast and hard, and it had snuck up on me like a thief in the night, stealing my heart away. I had slid down that slide at the speed of light and ended up intensely and irrevocably in love with Jack.

And now he's gone.

Grace has no qualms about grabbing the keys out of my hand and busting into Jack's apartment when he doesn't answer her incessant banging. I follow her in. A coffee cup sits on the table in front of the couch. A deep, dried stain clings to the bottom. But what's more interesting to me is that Jack's computer is sitting beside it. I plop down on the couch while Grace walks through the apartment. I open the computer and turn it on.

"This is a nice place," Grace says, resting her hip against the doorjamb of the bedroom. "I can see you living here."

"Any signs of life?"

"Well, there's dirty clothes in the hamper, and the bed is unmade."

"I made that bed on Sunday morning. So he was at least here Sunday night."

The computer makes its start-up noise, and I return my attention to it. I had planned to open the Internet browser and find the last site Jack had visited. But I don't know his password. So I log on as a guest user and get into my own email account. That way I can at least look at Jack's calendar.

"What day is it?" I ask Grace as I open the

calendar.

"Really? You *are* a giant mess," she quips.

"It's Saturday, right?"

"Yes, crazy. It's Saturday."

I look at today's schedule. "Oh my God! That's it! Nancy!"

"Nancy?" Grace asks.

"Jack and I were supposed to meet up with her and Trisha at a restaurant fifteen minutes ago."

"You think he went?"

"I don't know. But it's worth a try."

Suddenly, I lose my apathy. I'm as fired up to find Jack as Grace is now. Maybe more. I *do* want to tell him everything that happened at Morrison and Sons. I want to tell him I'm sorry. I want to *demand* he forgive me and take me back. For the first time in a week, I feel hope.

We make insanely good time as we plow through downtown traffic. Then Grace parks like a maniac, and we run into the restaurant. I practically fall over when I see Nancy and Trisha sitting on one side of a rectangular table. I move quickly past the tables of people, nearly getting clotheslined by a waitress on my way.

"Candace," Nancy says, standing as I approach.

I walk over and hug her. It's not how I would normally behave, especially toward a person I barely know. But then, I'm not myself these days in so many ways.

"Are you all right?" she asks me.

I turn to look at the woman still sitting at the table. I'd met Trisha before at Jack's office. And until I'd found out that she was Nancy's wife, she'd always kicked up my jealousy a notch. Without the youth of so many of the others I knew Jack thought of as kids, Trisha was drop-dead gorgeous with long, black hair and dark, smoky eyes.

"Nice to see you again, Trisha," I say, sitting down across from her because I'm not sure how much longer I can keep standing up.

She smiles at me. "Hi, Candace."

Nancy still looks confused, but she takes her seat next to Trisha. Grace follows suit, sitting beside me. I introduce Grace to them both.

"What's going on, Candace?" Nancy asks me after greeting Grace with a friendly smile.

"Have you seen Jack? Or talked to him?" I ask her.

"Not since Monday morning. He said he was going out of town for a while. He gave me a few instructions, and that was it. I haven't heard from him since. I kept trying to call, but I just got his voicemail. Trisha and I figured we'd show up here in hope he'd make an appearance."

I look around the restaurant. I don't know why. I know he's not here. I know he won't magically show up either. "He took off. We had a fight. More than a fight, really," I tell Nancy.

"What happened?"

Guilt pools in my stomach. "I've been working against you this whole time," I tell her. I can't look her in the eyes as I admit my treachery, so I focus my gaze on the salt and pepper shaker in the center of the table. "I got assigned to the Baldy project just after I met Jack. My job was to go through your application for historic status and find all the flaws. I did. And Hayden used my work to challenge the application."

I peek up at Nancy. She leans back in her chair and lets out a puff of air, her cheeks ballooning out as she does. "Oh, Candace."

I drop my eyes again and finish it. "I didn't tell Jack. The whole time we were sleeping together…building something…I kept it from him. I gave my two weeks' notice at work last Friday, and I figured as soon as my last day was over I'd tell him everything, and I'd help him fix it. I'd undo all the damage I'd done. But on Sunday, at brunch with the Morrisons, Hayden told Jack what I'd done. And he took off. He left me," I say, feeling the tears stinging my eyes at the words. I feel Grace's hand rub my back gently, and I look up at Nancy again, ready to face the music.

Nancy leans forward, her forearms resting on the table. "Candace, you work in a cutthroat business for a cutthroat company. You were a pawn in their game. You can't blame yourself for this."

"I like her," Grace says.

"But—" I protest.

"So, maybe he got pissed," Nancy says. "Jack does that. He flies off the handle. Believe me, I know. I love the man. But he's not always rational."

"Eventually, Jack will figure out this isn't your fault," Trisha says. "If he hasn't already."

I lean back in my seat and watch as the waitress brings Trisha and Nancy a second round of cocktails, then asks Grace and me if we want anything. I'm about to say no when Grace orders two mojitos.

After the waitress leaves, Grace turns to me. "Jack was so pissed at his family he took off for five years. And he got over that. He'll get over this, too, Candace."

"She has a point," Nancy says.

I look at her, knowing she is privy to this weird relationship, just like me. "I don't understand," I say. "The Morrisons seem like such nice, normal people. And Jack goes to freaking brunch with them every week. And they love him, Nancy. Really love him. I could see it. His mom and sister are crazy about him. And his dad. I mean, honestly, Nancy. I think his dad is actually *proud* of him."

"Honey, I've been trying to figure that family out for years. Don't waste your time," Nancy tells me. "Instead, let's concentrate on where the hell Jack might be."

****

We'd spent the next couple of hours discussing Jack's possible whereabouts. I concentrated on gleaning as much information as possible from Nancy and Trisha while Grace concentrated on polishing off several mojitos.

By the time I'd driven Grace's car back across the Bay to my apartment, with her practically passed out in the passenger's seat, I'd decided Jack had definitely gone to Rio.

Nancy and I had discussed Rio in detail. Apparently, Jack hadn't revealed his location during the missing five years to her until a few days ago. She'd told me he'd said opening up to me about it made him want to tell her, too.

But she didn't know any more than I did. The sum of the information we had was he'd stayed with an American named Menelaus whom he'd gone to college with and that Meno owned a restaurant down there. It wasn't much to go on. And without Meno's last name or the name of the restaurant, Google and I didn't get far last night as I tried to search on my computer.

So now it's Sunday morning, and I'm determined to go through with my plan. Grace is still with me. She's called Eric, who is God-knows-where in the world, and told him she's staying with me until we've completely fixed my love life.

We're headed back into the city this morning, Grace with a killer hangover and me with nerves of fire. We are going to talk to the Morrisons.

I'm in a strange state as I ring the doorbell. After Jack left last Sunday, Frances had been kind to me. I'd insisted on leaving right away, afraid I'd break down and cry at any moment. While John Sr. had been giving Hayden hell and Chelsea stared daggers at me, Frances had escorted me to the door. She'd asked me to stay and talk with her, but I'd refused, hightailing it out of there as fast as I could.

Now I am coming back to the Morrisons, hat in hand, asking for their help. But as nervous and embarrassed as I am, I'm also determined.

Chapter 18

"Candace," Jack's mother says, surprising me by opening the door.

"Hello, Mrs. Morrison. I'm sorry to disturb you at brunch, but—"

"You're not disturbing us. And call me Frances." She swings the door wide and extends her arm in welcome.

I walk into the foyer, Grace at my heels. "This is my friend, Grace. I hope you don't mind that I showed up unexpectedly and brought her along."

"Of course not. Nice to meet you, Grace." Frances extends her hand and Grace takes it, smiling.

"We didn't really have the heart to do the whole family brunch thing without Jack, and Hayden had an appointment anyway. So John, Chelsea, and I just grabbed a quick breakfast. But can I offer you something?"

"No, thank you," I say.

"Coffee would be amazing," my binge-drinking friend says.

"Of course." Frances moves into the living room and sits us both down on the couch while she asks Delia to bring coffee. Then she sits down across from us. "I'm hoping you've heard from Jack," she says.

"I'm afraid not. In fact, I was hoping *you'd* heard from him."

"John," she calls toward the hall. "Come in here, please."

John Sr. emerges. And for the first time ever, I see the man in casual clothing. He's wearing jeans and a Stanford sweatshirt. If I wasn't already sitting, I would fall over.

"Did you get any more texts from Jack?" Frances asks him the minute he's in the room.

"Hi, Candace," he says cordially, taking a seat on the chair beside his wife. "Just the one on Monday," he tells her.

"What did it say?" I ask.

"He said he was going to be out of town for a while and not to worry."

"And are you? Worried, I mean?" I ask him.

John Sr. runs a hand through his hair and leans back in the chair. "Always. But it won't get me anywhere. Jack is stubborn as hell."

Suddenly, I feel defensive. I don't truly understand Jack's relationship with his father. So I've never felt like I could judge it. But now I am. "He's a good man," I say vehemently.

John Sr. scrutinizes me for a long moment. Then he says, "Yes, he is, Candace. In fact, he's a better man than I raised him to be."

This statement takes me aback. And I can't seem to find words.

"Forgive me, I'm Grace, by the way. Candace's best friend," Grace says to John Sr., breaking into our awkward moment. "But didn't Jack come back after his college days and immediately start attacking your company, the company he was supposed to inherit?"

John Sr. turns his eyes to Grace. He has the same

look on his face I've seen him get in meetings with his staff. He is stern, dominating, and not to be trifled with.

But then he turns back to me, and his gaze softens. "Candace. You're important to Jack. So I'm going to tell you what he probably hasn't. I'm proud of everything he's done in his whole life, and I'm proud of the man he's become. I intend to change my company, perhaps more slowly than Jack likes. But that's a difference in philosophy. I am an experienced businessman who runs on logic. I know such a monumental change needs to take place organically, slowly. But Jack doesn't have my experience, and he doesn't think wholly with his head. He thinks with his heart. So, he's impatient. To the rest of the world, it might look like we're constantly butting heads. But that's not really the case. Jack pokes and prods at me. He does it because he cares about me and about the company. It's not as black and white as it looks from the outside."

"But you wanted me to spy on him," I accuse.

His brow knits up. "No. I wanted you to keep him out of jail. I want him safe. There are only so many ways to do that, but I will employ all the resources I have at my disposal to make that happen. If Garrity, or anyone else, asked you do anything other than that, it was *not* on my orders."

Frances turns her head abruptly, as though something has caught her attention. Then Chelsea makes her way into the room quietly. She perches herself on the ottoman at her father's feet.

John Sr. leans forward, resting his arms on his knees, and demands my attention. "I may not be open and cuddly about it. But if you're going to be as important a part of Jack's life as I suspect you are, you should know, I love my son, and I'd do anything for him."

"The five years he was gone were very hard," Frances says softly.

"He runs away when things get too hard. It's without a doubt his greatest flaw. So, Candace," John Sr. says, "what are you going to do to get him back here to San Francisco, and how can we help?"

I'm still feeling floored by everything he's just said, and it takes me a minute to wrap my head around it. While I'm silently reeling, Grace speaks. "We suspect he's gone to Rio again. Do you have any information about the person he stayed with when he went there last time, this Meno guy?"

"I'm afraid not. I had a private investigator look into him when Jack was gone before. He found out about his parents and his childhood. But the parents died in a car crash just before he left for Brazil, and other than Jack, we couldn't find any contacts in the States. So, the investigator ran dry when he tried to track him down."

I can feel myself deflating. I slump back on the couch and throw my head back, willing the tears to stay at bay.

"Chelsea," Frances says, pleading.

Chelsea makes a strange face.

"Chelsea, what do you know?" her father asks sternly.

"I might know something," she says shyly. Then she turns to me. She hitches her glasses up on her nose and her lips purse together into a thin line. "But why should I help you? You betrayed him."

"Chelsea!" Frances scolds.

"It's not that simple, Chels," John Sr. says.

Chelsea gives her father a strange look, one I don't understand at all. Then she turns back to me. "Jack keeps everyone at arm's length, except me and maybe Nancy. He tells me things. He trusts me. And then you walk into his life. And for some reason, he's crazy about you. I don't get it, but I could see it on his face. And I could see the hurt on his face when you betrayed him. Why should I help you?" she says, the emotion rich in her voice.

"Because he means a lot to me. And I want a chance to explain," I tell her.

"Explain it to *me* first," she demands.

"Chelsea," Frances tries again. But Chelsea keeps her laser focus on me.

I lean forward, giving Chelsea all my attention. "Okay. I'll explain." I take a deep breath, ready to admit all of it. "I took the job at Morrison before I met Jack, as you know. It was an amazing career opportunity for me, and I wanted nothing more than to succeed. Then I got assigned to Jack. And I didn't like it at first. In fact, it was a bit of a nightmare. *He* was a bit of a nightmare. But I got to know Jack, and I fell for him, fast and hard."

Chelsea watches me as if she's trying to memorize each move on my face. I stay focused on telling the story the best I can and continue. "It went against all my ethics to have a relationship with him. In my mind, Jack was my client. And I suspect in your father's mind, he was, too. So it was wrong of me to be with him romantically, but I couldn't help how I felt. I thought a lot about quitting, and Jack and I discussed it.

As you know, things moved pretty fast with us, and I hadn't really figured out what to do. In the meantime, I worked on the Baldy project. I'd gotten the assignment before I knew much about it, and before...before Jack and I...became what we are."

"But when you started dating, why didn't you tell him?"

"I had moments where I almost did. But I'd signed a nondisclosure agreement when I started at Morrison. And I would be chalking up more unethical behavior if I did that, not to mention setting myself up to be sued. I was in a real bind, Chelsea. And each time I came close to telling Jack, he would assure me I didn't need to tell him what I was doing at work. He didn't want to complicate matters any worse than they already were. We were both trying to do *something* right in all of this." I take another deep breath and admit, right in front of my old boss's boss, "I would have told him after my last day at Morrison. It would have been the first thing I did."

"I wanted Hayden to learn for himself," John Sr. interjects. "I fully expected him to fail at the Baldy project and for Jack to get the historic designation. Hayden would be forced to come up with some other solution. I had hoped he and Jack would work it out. Hands-off approach. It's how I've tried to sort things out between them since they were kids. Watch closely, but don't interfere too much. I never saw this kind of wrinkle coming."

"So you love him?" Chelsea asks me.

I swallow hard and slowly, I nod.

"But you don't even know each other that well. I mean, you can't, right? It's only been a few weeks."

I shrug. "Doesn't matter. It happened. And I can't undo it. I wouldn't if I could."

Chelsea is still staring at me when her father says, "Chelsea, tell us what you know."

Her eyes stay locked on mine. "He told me the name of Meno's restaurant once and I Googled it. Give me your phone. I'll pull it up."

Chapter 19

Present day—Rio

"Bob's North American Restaurant. Really?" Grace says, her nose all scrunched up as she looks at the sign.

I ignore her. She's already gone off on this four or five times since Chelsea told us the name, despite the fact that Chelsea had explained that according to Jack, Meno was trying to make it sound quintessentially USA. "Menelaus's North American Restaurant" just didn't have the same feel.

I don't really care what the name of the damned restaurant is. I am much more concerned with the man who may or may not be in it. I'm also a little worried I'm going to fall asleep at any moment.

Sunday afternoon, Jack's father had arranged a flight to Rio on a corporate jet. After gathering up some clothes and our passports, we boarded the plane around midnight. The fourteen-hour flight and four-hour time difference had us landing in Rio at eight p.m., where a private car had whisked us away to the heart of the city and deposited us here.

I'm exhausted, anxious, and a little terrified. Grace is none of these things, and she boldly steps in front of the floor to ceiling windows of the restaurant and peers in like a creeper. A few feet away, I hide in the shadow of the building next door.

"Oh my, that has to be him. Candace, he is *delicious*. If I wasn't married and he wasn't yours..."

I steel myself and move to stand beside Grace, fully aware I'm now exposed for everyone in the restaurant to see. My eyes sweep from closest to us, to farthest away, across the large open room. It's pretty busy for a Monday night, and most of the tables are filled with diners. Wait staff and busboys move fluidly among the sitting patrons. My gaze crosses the hostess station and the absolutely beautiful woman standing there and lands on the large oak bar in the far corner.

There's an older Brazilian man standing behind the end of the bar closest to the door, his hair caught up in a ponytail that swings from side to side as he moves around pouring drinks. And beside him is Jack.

Apart from being the palest face in the joint, he also stands out because he is so stunningly handsome. The minute I catch sight of him, I want to burst into the room and run into his arms. But, of course, I don't.

I watch him for a moment. His hands are quick and lithe as he flips glasses up and mixes drinks with an artistic flair and confident ability. God, is there anything Jack isn't good at?

"I'm going to get a drink," Grace says, turning on her heel and marching toward the door.

"Grace, wait," I call in a loud whisper. But she ignores me, wrenching open the door and holding it for me, a pointed look on her face.

I follow her in like a timid kitten, fighting the urge to flee. She walks up to the hostess with a look of purpose.

"May I help you?" the ridiculously beautiful

woman asks in English spiced with a sexy accent.

"We're just going to the bar," Grace says, airily. "I want to talk to that one." She points at Jack.

"Who doesn't?" the hostess says. "Good luck with that. He's got a girlfriend back in the States, and he's a damned saint about it."

Grace turns to me and raises one eyebrow. Then she begins the trek to the bar. Helplessly, I follow.

As we're approaching, a man emerges from the back hallway. He's clearly an American. He's multiracial, like me. Only he's Caucasian and Arabic, I think. He wears a pair of jeans and an SF Giants jersey. And he has that wide-stride, cocky walk down pat. This must be Meno.

Grace and I approach slowly, but Jack never looks at us. Instead, he responds to something Meno says by following the man back down the hallway he emerged from. And just like that, he's gone again.

Undeterred, Grace stops in front of the bar and leans over, her arms resting on the glossy surface. I stand behind her, feeling completely out of my skin.

"Hi, ladies," the other bartender says, greeting us. "What can I get you?"

"I want to talk to Jack Morrison." Grace hooks her thumb over her shoulder, gesturing to the direction in which Jack disappeared. "Where did he go?"

The bartender shrugs. "Meno wanted to talk to him about something. They're probably in the office." Then he moves over to attend to another patron.

Grace whirls around, nearly knocking me over because I'm cowering into her back at this point. Then she just walks toward the hallway.

I grab her arm. "Wait, we can't just go back there."

"Sure we can." She rounds the corner of the hallway and heads toward the door at the far end.

"Grace," I whisper. "What are you going to do, just barge in there?"

"No, I'll knock," she practically shouts as we near the door. A small metal sign on the door says Office.

Grace doesn't end up knocking. She doesn't have to. Meno must have heard her loud-ass voice because as we reach the door, he swings it open.

And we stand there—Meno, Grace, and I—staring at each other. I move my eyes just a little to the left and there is Jack, sitting on the edge of Meno's desk. His arms rest at his sides, his palms flat on the metal surface. Our eyes lock, and I am completely immobilized.

"You must be Candie," Meno says.

"She is. And I'm Grace."

"I'm Meno. It's nice to meet you," he purrs.

Meno moves his head from side to side and looks between Jack and me. "You know, gorgeous Grace, why don't you and I get a drink?"

"She's married," Jack says, his eyes staying on me.

"Doesn't mean I can't buy the lady a drink." Meno holds out his arm, and Grace loops hers through it. She gives my hand a squeeze as she and Meno leave, but I can't look at her. I'm too busy staring at Jack.

I can't read his expression, and I feel the tears pushing their way through my skull. So I move into the room and turn around, closing the door firmly behind me. When I spin back around, Jack is moving toward me.

Just as the tears start to streak down my face, he pulls me into his arms. I am so happy to be here—right here—my face pressed against his hard chest, his arms wrapped around me. But it doesn't seem to matter how happy Jack's embrace makes me because the sobbing gets worse.

At some point, Jack pulls me across the room to a small couch. He sits down and settles me into his lap fluidly. I press my face into the crook of his neck. He smells amazing. And his hand rubs languidly along my back. With his other hand, he plays with my hair.

My sobbing slows, and I take heavy breaths, listening to the sound of Jack breathing. If I can quiet myself, I can hear his heart beating. It is a very comforting sound.

Once I'm still, Jack kisses the top of my head. "I can't believe you came all the way here for me," he whispers.

"I'd do more than that," I mumble into his neck.

"God, I missed you."

I move my head so I can look into his beautiful blue eyes. He puts a hand on my cheek and gently wipes away a tear with his calloused thumb. I shiver at the sensation.

"I'm sorry, Jack."

He shakes his head. "You don't have anything to apologize for."

"But I should explain."

"No, Candie. I understand why you did what you did. I can't say I would have done anything different if I were in your shoes. You were caught between a rock and a hard place." He rests his forehead against mine. "I'm sorry I ran."

"That's what you do, right? You run and I cry."

He chuckled. "That's us, all right."

"But next time, take me with you."

"Definitely." Jack takes a deep breath. "I can't believe you came all the way here for me," he says again.

"Your dad helped. He sent us out here on a corporate jet." I run my hand through Jack's hair. It's soft and silky, and I love the way it feels threading through my fingers. "He loves you, Jack. And he's trying to change the company, to do the right thing."

"I know that, Candie. But I don't want to talk about my dad right now. I want to talk about *you*. What have you been doing for the last week?"

"Rotting in my apartment. I didn't even go to work. I just sat around feeling depressed, crying, and eating a lot of ice cream."

Jack pulls my face up gently, touching the tip of his nose to mine. "I'm so sorry, baby. And I'm sorry I waited so long. I have a flight booked for the morning. But I shouldn't have waited so long. I shouldn't have put you through all that."

"You were coming back?"

"Yes. I couldn't stay away from you any longer. I was just biding my time a little so I could figure out what to say to convince you to give me another chance."

"You thought you'd have to talk me into it? That's crazy, Jack."

He smiles and kisses me softly. I want to attack him, but I hold back. Because I like that we're talking. I like that we're working things out. The sex can wait, maybe not long, but for a while anyway.

"I think you should come back on the corporate jet with me. And before you argue, you should know, it

197

has a bedroom in the back."

Jack laughs at me and moves one hand to my thigh. "Actually, I'd rather stay here with you, show you the sights. I think you'd like Rio."

"That sounds nice."

"But…we should get Grace back. And we have work to do."

I nod. "Yes. I'm going to save the Baldy building, Jack."

****

"You were right. This *is* better," Jack says, running a finger down my ribs.

I nestle farther into his arms. "See, being rich can have its perks."

It's true. We lay on the bed in the little private cabin in the back of the corporate jet. Meanwhile, Grace and her new best friend, Meno, eat sushi and drink wine in the front of the plane. I'm glad Meno decided to join us for the long flight back to California to wrap up a few things with his parents' estate. I'm glad for purely selfish reasons. He can entertain Grace while Jack and I snuggle alone in the back of the plane.

"You realize, though, if you're going to work for me, we will never be rich," Jack says, pushing a lock of hair away from my cheek and giving me a guilty smile.

"Yes, I realize that. And like I told you, I changed my mind about absolutely everything lately, including my desire to be rich. *But* that doesn't mean I won't take advantage of your dad being rich when he offers to buy me things, or pay for fancy plane rides, or whatever."

"Hmmm," he mumbles, kissing my forehead. "To be negotiated at a future date."

"It's too bad we didn't have time to see more of

Rio," I muse.

In fact, we hadn't seen any of Rio. We'd helped close down the restaurant for the night. By then, it was late, and we'd gone straight back to Meno's place where I had promptly fallen asleep. We'd boarded this plane the next morning.

"Maybe in a couple months, we'll come back and stay for a little vacation," he suggests.

"Jack?"

"Hmmm?"

"I can't wait to run away with you."

Chapter 20

Two months later—San Francisco
Jack

"I want my lawyer," I say stoically.

Trent laughs. I look up at him. He and I were in Little League together twenty years ago. Now he's a cop, and I'm his prisoner.

"You sure you really want that, Jack?" He smirks.

I narrow my eyes at him. He's standing on the opposite side of the table I sit at in this dark, crappy, little room. "Are you denying me my rights, Trent?"

"Hell, no." He chuckles. "Your lawyer's already here. Your buddy Nancy must have called her. She's in the lobby. And she looks pissed."

I run my hand through my hair and try to put on a brave face. "Good. If she's here, I'd like to see her."

Trent laughs again. "Your funeral, man."

Trent leaves for a few minutes, and I am alone. The chain hangs down between my wrists as I rest my forehead on the heels of my hands. I know this is going to be painful. But I got myself into this mess. I have to take my licks.

She comes in like a storm. Her anger is punctuated by the click of her heels, hard and fast on the concrete flooring. "We don't need an audience," she snaps at Trent.

"But, ma'am—"

"Out!"

The door shuts, and we are alone.

Even pissed off, she's gorgeous. She wears a light purple suit and heels. Her hair is up in a tidy bun, and her face is carefully made up. She'd been at a conference with my father this afternoon, and I imagine that's where she was when she got the call from Nancy. I wonder idly if my father is also out in the lobby of the police station.

She pulls out the chair across from me roughly, scraping the floor with a loud shriek. Then, she sits down delicately on the edge of the chair while throwing her briefcase on the table with a harsh *thunk*.

"You said you were holding a peaceful demonstration at the Capitol about homelessness," she says in a low voice, enunciating each and every word. Her eyes penetrate me, and her lips are tight.

"I was, baby."

"Do not call me 'baby' when you're wearing handcuffs, John Morrison Jr.!"

There's a BDSM joke in there, but I don't dare make it. The use of my full name indicates I am in more trouble than I was the time I went joyriding in my parents' car at fifteen and got it stuck on the beach in high tide.

"I can explain everything."

"Oh, you're going to, Jack." She leans over the table menacingly. I reach for her hands, but she pulls away from me.

"What did Nancy tell you?" I ask.

"Not much, she didn't get a chance. Here's what I was told by the assistant DA. I was told you are being charged with issuing a threat, and that the man pressing the charges is Mr. Grover. As I recall, that is the very man you promised me and your father you'd stay the hell away from. That criminal charge can carry up to a year in county jail, Jack!"

I lean back in my seat and take a deep breath. "That's what he claims, yeah. Do you want to hear my side of the story?"

Candie lets out a breath of her own, and her shoulders sag. "Yes. Of course, I do. Tell me what happened."

Candie doesn't work for me. My father made her the head of a new department at the company dealing exclusively with renovating historic properties. She navigates the red tape and ensures all the paperwork is in good shape. Candie says it's best we don't work together; it would put our relationship under too much stress.

When he stole her away from Homes Without Inc., my dad donated to the lawyer fund, which allowed us to hire someone else. But Candie doesn't trust anyone else with my freedom, so she is here now, representing me herself. I have a feeling *that* is definitely going to create stress on our relationship.

"We were at the demonstration—the legal demonstration I told you about this morning—and Grover comes waltzing out of the capitol building waving his newest permit in our faces and taunting us. I kept everyone under control at first. But then he got in his car, and he pulled right up to us and started in again. Juanita got upset and lost her shit. She threw herself in front of his car."

At this point in the story, Candie's face softens and

concern begins to overtake anger.

"So Grover inches up, just enough to trap her shoe under his tire," I continue.

Candie gasps. "Is she okay?"

I nod. "Yes, but she was trapped there, in a very dangerous situation. So I ran over to his driver's side window and shouted."

"What did you shout?"

"Who the hell knows, really? I'm sure I told him to back up. And I'm sure there were a lot of swear words in there, maybe a threat." I shrug. "Who knows? I was protecting Juanita. I was pissed."

Candie takes several deep breaths, closing her eyes. When she opens them again, I can see she is composed, professional, and deeply, deeply worried. "That is, of course, not the story Grover is telling."

"I have witnesses."

She nods. "Yes. And that's a good thing. But they are definitely one-sided witnesses, Jack."

I grinned. "So, I guess Nancy didn't get a chance to tell you the whole thing was recorded?"

"What?"

"Yep. She's got the whole thing on her phone's camera."

She stands up. "That's great, Jack. I can get this taken care before you are even arraigned."

"Candie, wait." I grab her hand. "I don't want that."

"What?"

"I don't want anyone to know about the video...yet."

She slumps down in the chair. "Jack...what are you saying?"

"I want it to go forward. My arraignment. Even jail. I don't want you, or my dad, to post bail. I want this thing to go big. Then, at just the right moment, we release the video. The charges will be dropped—"

"Maybe."

"They *will* be. And we will have brought attention to Grover and all the shit he's getting away with."

Candie hangs her head and places a hand over her eyes. She's let me keep hold of her other hand, and I rub slow circles on her palm.

Finally, she looks up at me. "This is what you want?"

I nod.

"You could have told me, Jack. We could have discussed it."

"I didn't plan it, Candie. The opportunity just arrived. And now that it's here…"

Her eyes sparkle with a wetness that scares me. "You want to get arraigned, and you want to go to jail?"

I nod again.

She pulls her hand out of mine and stands up again. "Fine. See you at the arraignment."

And then she is gone.

****

It's been twenty hours since I pleaded not guilty at my arraignment. Candie sat beside me, but she didn't so much as glance my way. And she wouldn't let me touch her, not once. When it was over, she walked right out of the courtroom, practically dragging my parents with her.

Now I have my first visitor, and it's not Candie.

"Are you all right?" Nancy asks me.

"Yeah. I'm fine."

"I brought you some things."

"Thanks, Nance. I appreciate it. Um...did you talk to Candie?"

She nods. "Yeah. She brought the stuff to the office, and we talked."

"Did she move out of our apartment? Is she leaving me?"

"Don't be ridiculous, Jack. She's pissed at you, but she hasn't abandoned you."

My sense of relief at her words is not quite complete. I believe Nancy, I do. But I'd rather hear it from Candie's lips. And so far, I haven't heard a thing from her.

"So, how's our plan coming?"

"Good. Very good. Your arrest is all over the media. And Grover is running around telling everyone his side of the story. Meanwhile, the DA is on TV talking about throwing the book at you. The situation is getting riper. I'm going to give a press conference in the morning where we talk about the two-dozen people Grover just put out on the street with his new project. Then, we'll wait another day or two and put out the video."

"Good strategy."

"It was your dad's idea."

"What?" I ask, deeply shocked.

"He came up with it."

"Wait. What?"

Nancy chuckles. "After you were arrested and you talked to Candace, we all went back to the office. I showed them the video, and we talked about the importance of taking advantage of this situation to save people's homes. They both seemed really into it, to tell you the truth. That's when your dad came up with this idea."

"And Candie? What did she think of the strategy?"

"She was on board," she says. But that doesn't mesh with how she'd treated me yesterday in the courtroom. "I have to tell you, Jack. Even though I think we'll get great media coverage and Grover will be forced to drop the charges, it could take a while. You might be in for as long as a week."

"I can hack it, Nancy. What did Candie say when she gave you my things?"

"She asked me to make sure you're all right."

"Meaning she's not planning to come by."

"Pretty much," she says softly.

****

Nancy had been right. It did take a while to get me released. In fact, it took thirteen long days. The publicity went exactly as we'd planned. In fact, it was better than we'd hoped. But Grover had held out as long as he could before dropping the charges against me. Then the DA had waited as long as he could before actually releasing me.

Candie came to see me a few times, always as my lawyer, always with someone else in tow, and always with a cold, hard demeanor. When I walked out of the jail, I expected to find her there, still angry probably, distant maybe, but definitely there. Only she wasn't.

It was my dad who picked me up. It turned out to be a bit of a media circus. It would probably cause him trouble in the long run because there was speculation my war on Grover was related to my father being a business competitor with Grover. But my dad didn't care. He was relieved to have me out. And I was pretty pleased to see him, too.

John Morrison Sr. has always been a man of few words, choosing instead to say only what had to be said. But he doesn't shut up on the car ride from the jail to my apartment. He talks about the finesse with which Nancy and I played the system to bring attention to the plight of disadvantaged people who are losing their homes for nothing but greed. He chats excitedly about how he'd come up with his idea for the strategy and how it was based on both his knowledge of Grover and his own business acumen. I grin ear to ear listening to him. For the last seven years, I'd dreamed of having a conversation like this with my dad.

"Jack, what you did was really brave," my father says.

I don't really know how to respond to his praise. "I bet Mom is pissed," I say casually.

"She was worried about you. That's why I wouldn't let her come visit you in jail."

"Wise choice."

"She would have completely freaked out," he says, chuckling.

I laugh at my dad. He's like a whole new person. And I can't wait to get to know him again.

He drops me off at my apartment. Before I step out of the car, he places a hand on my shoulder. "Good luck, son."

"Thanks, Dad. I think I'm going to need it."

He chuckles. "I think you are, too."

I walk quickly up the steps to the building and make my way to the elevator. I'm desperate to see Candie. I need to hold her in my arms, to feel her body against mine. I just hope she'll let me.

When I walk in the door, the apartment is still. The clean kitchen and tidy living room make my chest tighten. Nancy had assured me Candie hadn't moved out. And my dad seemed certain she would be here, but suddenly I am filled with doubt.

I walk through the place slowly, listening to the rubber soles of my sandals as they grip and release the wood flooring. I drop the plastic bag filled with my personal items on the couch and follow the sound of soft music coming from the den.

We've rearranged the room, adding an additional desk that sits perpendicular to mine. We've also added a few of Candie's personal touches, all the while retaining the retro-style we both like so much.

She's sitting at her desk with her back to me, typing away on her laptop. Her iPod is docked on my desk, the music low enough that it doesn't mask my footsteps. But she doesn't turn around. I stand behind her, unsure if I should dare touch her.

The clicking of her fingers on the keyboard stops. She snaps the laptop shut and turns around to face me. Still seated, she looks up into my eyes.

I drop down onto my knees in front of her. "Hey, baby."

I hold my breath, waiting. Then she stands, and I follow suit. Her eyes travel up and down my body, examining me. She makes a circle motion with her finger, and I know what she wants, so I turn around, letting her see me from all sides. When I'm facing her again, she says, "Take off your shirt."

I hesitate, knowing it will only upset her. But chances are good she already knows about my injury. She's my lawyer. She probably got a call. Her eyes narrow. Instead of risking further wrath, I just pull the T-shirt over my head and throw it on the back of her chair.

She stares at the fist-shaped purple bruise just below my ribs on my right side. It came from an asshole who'd punched me while I stood in line for dinner, for no reason other than he felt like it. It's a few days old now and starting to fade.

I'd thought about trying to delay my release just so I could have more time to heal before Candie saw it. And I almost wish I had when I see tears cloud her eyes. She reaches her hand toward the bruise, and I catch it. I pull it up to my chest and press it to my heart while at the same time taking a step closer to her.

"I missed you so much," I tell her.

She looks up at me and swallows back her tears. "This was very, very hard, Jack."

"I know, baby. I'm sorry," I whisper.

She shakes her head. "No, you're not. You got exactly what you wanted out of it."

I don't have a response to this. I squeeze her hand, but she pulls away and begins to pace in front of me. She takes two steps in one direction, pivots, and takes two steps in the other direction. She watches her feet while she walks. "I know you did the right thing, Jack. I won't argue that point. In fact, I'm happy with the outcome myself. Homes Without Inc. achieved its goals as an organization. And just like you, I am passionate about that. But—"

She stops pacing and plants her feet, pointing a finger toward my chest. "It doesn't change the fact that we didn't make this decision together. *You* made it, Jack. And I had to live with the consequences. I didn't get a chance to digest it or analyze it or think about all the things that could have gone wrong." I watch her anger flare as she goes over the same thing she told me when she came to visit me in jail that second time. "If you had been convicted, it would have been a strike, Jack. As in the three-strikes law in California. *And* it could have meant up to a year in prison, Jack. A year!"

I just nod.

Candie stops and takes a deep breath. We're facing each other again, and she's just a few inches away. If I reach out, I can pull her to me. But I don't. I wait.

"I was scared," she says softly. "I lay in our bed alone every night and wondered what was happening to you. I wanted to see you, but seeing you in jail…"

I finally reach out to her, and she comes willingly as I pull her against me. I bury my face in her hair and breathe in her scent as she grips my back and presses against my chest. "I'm sorry," I whisper.

"Just…let's be more prepared next time, okay?" she says, sniffing lightly.

"Next time?"

"I'm not an idiot, Jack. I know there will be a next time."

"I don't plan on it, sweetheart."

"Not jail," she says. "But *something*. You'll do something that is not necessarily the most cautious and well thought out. You'll do something, in your pursuit of truth and justice, that I would prefer you not do."

"But you'll still be around for that, right?" I ask nervously.

Candie pulls away from me enough to look up into my eyes. "Yes, Jack. I'll be here. I accept who you are. Your passion. Your determination. Your freaking stubbornness. It's all part of you, and I love you. All of you. Even when you are a complete pain in the ass."

I bend down and kiss her. It is soft and tender, and absolutely perfect for the moment. I have waited so long for this, I don't feel the need to rush it now I'm here and we're alone. I pull back just enough to speak. "So...I'm forgiven?"

"For now," she says, her voice low and seductive.

Chapter 21

Four months later—San Francisco

Nancy bursts into my office just as I'm hanging up the phone. I lean back in my chair and watch her saunter across the room until she comes to rest beside my desk, her hip leaning up against it.

"What's up?" I ask her.

"When are you doing it?"

"Doing what?"

Nancy opens the top right drawer of my desk and looks pointedly at the little felt box nestled inside.

"You've been rifling through my office?" I ask, not nearly as surprised as I sound.

"You always say it's a safe place." She gestures toward the chairs and couches that take up the majority of the room.

She's right, of course. I hold meetings with employees in here, and I always start them the same way, by saying this is a safe place to say anything. But I roll my eyes at her anyway.

"Did you look at it?" I ask her, nodding toward the box.

"Yes. And it's gorgeous. Did you pick it out all by yourself? Because I have to say, if you did, I'm impressed."

"You think I don't have taste?"

She eyes my jeans and sandals before saying bluntly, "No."

"Okay, I admit it. I took Chelsea. She helped me pick it out."

"I can't believe you didn't ask me," she pouts, shutting the drawer for emphasis.

"Chelsea knows Candie."

My statement only makes it worse, and she crosses her arms over her chest.

"You know what I mean."

My sister and Candie have become very close in the last few months. They created a bond almost as quickly as Candie and I did. And I wondered if that was just the way it was with Candie. She has the power to grab hold of people and steal their hearts within moments of meeting her.

"So…when are you going to ask? More important, *how* are you going to ask?"

I run my hand through my hair. It's getting really long, almost ready for a ponytail—that's what Candie says. She teases me about it, but I know she secretly loves it. That's the main reason I haven't cut it.

"I don't know. Every time I come up with an idea, I scrap it. Candie deserves something special. And this won't be the first time she's been proposed to, you know. Hey, where is she anyway?" I ask, looking nervously at the door.

Candie was over at our office earlier this morning, along with one of Hayden's minions. They picked up a couple of my staffers to take with them to a meeting with the head of the Housing Authority. She'd brought me a cup of coffee from the little shop across the street. Candie and I plan to buy the place in a couple of months. The owner is going to give us a good price because he wants to retire. We plan to hire locals down on their luck to staff it. All the profits will go to charities fighting human trafficking.

I remember the suit she was wearing. She looked freaking amazing. The thought gives me a jealous twinge. She looks like a goddess right now, and she's meeting with a young, good-looking, rising political star. But I shake it off. Candie loves me, jeans, long hair, and all.

"So give me some advice. How should I do it?"

"I suggest you propose while you're doing your favorite thing to do together."

I raise my eyebrow. "You think I should propose in bed."

Nancy rolls her eyes. "Okay, your second favorite thing. Think about it. Pick an activity you both enjoy, when you're happy and relaxed, and that is something you always do together." She pushes off the desk and starts walking toward the door. "And keep your mind out of the gutter." Nancy is about to open the door when she whirls back around. "Oh, I forgot the reason I actually came in here. Hayden called while you were on the phone. He wants you to call him back. He said it's urgent."

"What isn't urgent with my brother these days. You know, I almost miss the apathetic party boy he once was."

Nancy smirks and leaves the office while I reach for the phone.

"Hey, big brother," Hayden says when he answers.

Our relationship is significantly better these days. When I first got back from Rio with Candie, Hayden wouldn't even talk to me. And he was really pissed when Candie pushed the historic designation on the Baldy building through. But I went down to his office every day for two weeks until he finally agreed to have a cup of coffee with me. I shared my vision for the Baldy building with him. And each time we went out to talk, I grew the vision a little more. I started to show him how he could be the hero in this story, turning the building into a beautiful and profitable landmark for the city while housing low-income people.

Hayden eventually came around, and the project is going well. My next step is to talk to my brother about our relationship. But that will take more time.

"What's going on?" I ask him.

"I think you and I both know I didn't pay much attention while I was getting that college degree. And Kent just dropped off some paperwork I can't make heads or tails of. The dude's a total douchebag, and I am *not* asking him to help me. So…"

"You need a lawyer, not me."

"Yep."

"Pretty sure that's why Candie works for you, man."

"I plan to ask her for her help. But I wanted to make sure you were cool with it."

This is weird. "Why the hell wouldn't I be?"

"I don't know. I mean, she's your fiancée, and you can be kinda…"

And then I get it. This is not because he's running Candie's help by me. He knows better than that. He called me because he found out I bought the ring.

"Chelsea told you."

Hayden laughs. "I made her. She had that smug

'I'm keeping a secret' look on her face when I was at the house yesterday. So I tickled her until she cried uncle and told me."

"You are a terrible big brother. I am so much better at it than you."

"You always were. So, did you do it yet?"

"Not yet. But since the whole freaking world knows, I guess I better do it soon before you all wreck the surprise."

****

Nancy is a genius. After her suggestion yesterday, I'd thought about the things Candie and I liked to do together. When I had an epiphany about the perfect thing, I insisted we both bug out of work early today. It's Friday, and Candie is exhausted from spending the morning explaining a bunch of shit to Hayden, so she easily agreed.

She wasn't suspicious as we headed over the Bay Bridge or when we made our way to the Redwood Regional Park. After all, we do this all the time. It's something that is just for us, our quiet time.

Candie and I spend time with our families, we go out with friends, we travel, too. But our favorite times are when it's just the two of us. Whether it's hanging out in our apartment or walking through the giant trees, we revel in just being together.

Now we're walking in the woods on a slightly chilly, gray day. It's quiet in the park because of the weather, and we walk along the path undisturbed. I stop underneath the same tree where I kissed her on that fateful Sunday.

"Candie," I ask, pulling her into my arms. "Are you happy?"

She smiles at me and puts her hand on my beard. I've been growing it for a few weeks, and Candie says I look like one of the hippies she spent her life refusing to date. But she likes it. She likes to run her hand over it.

"God, yes, Jack. I'm so happy." She reaches up and kisses me gently on the lips.

"Good. Because I have a question to ask you."

"Are you going to ask me to marry you, Jack?"

Stunned into silence, all I can think is Chelsea has ratted me out. But Candie continues, "Because if you're not, I'm going to tell you to table whatever it was you were going to say, and *I'm* going to ask *you* to marry *me*."

"Um…" I'm feeling overwhelmed. So I just ask the most immediate question. "Did Chelsea say something?"

Her brow wrinkles for a second. Then, she shakes her head. "I didn't know what you were going to say. But this is the perfect time and the perfect place. And if you won't ask me, then I'll ask you, because Jack, I want to be with you forever." A tear slips out of her left eye. But this time it's a happy tear.

"I guess we're thinking exactly the same thing, baby." I pull the ring box out of my pocket. "So I suppose you can have this."

I pop open the box, and Candie gazes at the ring, a massive smile taking up her face. She snatches the ring from the box and holds it up to the light for a better look. Then she looks at me. "Put it on me, Jack," she demands.

"Yes, ma'am."

I take the ring from her and slip it onto her finger.

Then I shove the empty box in my pocket and wrap my arms back around her. She looks up and begs me for a kiss with her eyes. So I lean down and give it to her.

Epilogue

Six years later—San Francisco

I walk into the room quietly, the tread from my stocking feet barely a whisper on the hardwood floors. She doesn't see me approaching. She still thinks I'm in the den, on the phone with my father.

My wife is caught red-handed right now, only she doesn't know it yet. She's on the couch. Her back rests against the arm, and her legs are stretched out in front of her. And there, on her lap, is Lenny. His grayish-white coat is rumpled from what was clearly a recent petting session. His head rests on her tummy, the hair over his eyes flopped down, hiding his contentment. He lets out a little satisfied puff of air as she pulls on one ear.

"I knew it," I say.

Startled, Candie looks up from the book she's reading. Her eyes are wide as she gazes at me, then she glances down at the dog in her lap. And when she looks back up, she's guilty.

She doesn't move Lenny, and she doesn't stop the gentle stroking of his ear as I round the couch and kneel in front of her, so we're face to face.

"You pretended all this time to dislike the poor little guy, and here you are," I accuse. I can't hide the amusement in my tone.

"I didn't say I didn't like him," she says.

"Really?" I use my fingers to make a list of her offences. "You said he was too big, even though he only weighs sixteen pounds. You said he was too old, even though we have no idea how old he really is. You said he had too much fur, even though he has enough poodle in there somewhere that he doesn't really shed much. *And* you said he was ugly."

Candie looks down at Lenny, still perfectly happy in her lap, and clearly unaware of her grievances against him. He wags his tail lazily and licks her hand. She shrugs. "I was wrong. He's adorable."

I lean forward and kiss her quickly.

"But," she says, as I lean back, "the timing was bad."

I can't argue with that. We'd picked up the abandoned mixed-breed mutt at the pound thinking we had years to get used to him, and him to us. But just a few months later, we've discovered that for all three of us, things are going to be completely upended.

I am about to respond to her with something comforting, when there is a knock on the door. As I get up, Candie does, too. She tucks Lenny into the crook of her arm. "I'll put him in the den," she says before walking down the hall.

Lenny was doing all right with visitors until recently. In fact, it was his changed behavior, a new protectiveness over Candie, that led us to investigate the cause.

Pushing Lenny's revelations out of my head, I walk to the door. When I open it, I am confronted with my sister, Chelsea. Her hair is messy, the skin around her eyes is bright red, and she's sniffing. She's a mess. And she isn't even supposed to be in San Francisco. What the hell is this?

"Chels, what's going on?" I ask her.

When she doesn't answer, I wrap my arms around her and pull her into the apartment. She buries her face in my chest. I am in physical pain seeing her like this. So I take her over to the couch and sit her down.

"Hey, Candie. Baby, can you come in here?" I call, feeling like whatever is happening, I definitely can't handle it by myself.

Candie reemerges from the den, where she's deposited Lenny. She takes a look at Chelsea and me and asks, "What's going on?"

"I don't know yet," I tell her.

"I'll make some tea," Candie says softly.

I sit with Chelsea as Candie goes into the living room. She's not speaking. So I decide to just wait until she's ready. I gently rub on her arm and hold her until Candie returns and sets a steaming mug of tea in front of Chelsea. Then she sits down in the chair across from us and leans forward.

Candie smiles at Chelsea. "Are you all right, sweetie?"

"I'm so glad you married my brother," Chelsea tells her.

"Me, too," Candie says, her eyes glancing up at me for a moment, before looking back at Chelsea. "That's how I got you as a sister."

Chelsea sits up and reaches for the mug Candie left for her. "I suppose you guys are wondering what I'm doing here."

"Yeah, actually, we thought you were supposed to be headed to LA this weekend," I tell her. She's been serving as the camera operator on a show for the last several months, and I know that the next stop on the schedule is the City of Angels.

She nods. "I'm supposed to be there right now. In fact, I'm probably going to get fired over this."

This surprises the hell out of me. Chelsea is very responsible. So I try to find the silver lining. "Well, that's okay. I mean, the show was going to be done soon anyway, right?"

"Yeah, but it was a hit, and I guess I can kiss next season goodbye," she says on a heavy sigh.

"What happened to make you leave your job?" I ask her.

"I can guess," Candie says. We both look up at her expectantly. "The same thing that made me leave mine once. A man. Am I right?"

Chelsea nods.

For a moment, I'm confused. Then it hits me. "Oh shit," I say, "not…"

"Yes, him," Chelsea confirms.

"I thought you were just friends," I say, the shock clear in my voice.

"You are so naïve," Candie says to me, shaking her head.

"Well, what happened?" I ask.

"It's a long story," Chelsea says.

Candie tucks one foot beneath her butt and leans back. The movement makes the little bump, that at this point in time only Lenny and I know about, stick out just the tiniest bit. She tells Chelsea, "I think you better start from the beginning."

A word about the author...

Kay Harris has had a diverse career with jobs ranging from college professor to park ranger. Now she adds author to her repertoire. Kay writes romance novels that contain a little bit of sweet, a dash of sexy, a touch of heartbreak, and a whole lot of fun!

Kay grew up in the Midwest and has since lived all over the western United States including Montana, Wyoming, Utah, Arizona, Nevada, and California. She loves to hike, is obsessed with museums, and enjoys taking her extremely tall and very handsome husband on adventures.

http://kayharrisauthor.com

On Twitter: @KayHarrisAuthor

On Facebook: AuthorKayHarris